ALSO BY J.L. JARVIS

Cedar Creek

Christmas at Cedar Creek
Snowstorm at Cedar Creek

Pine Harbor

Allison's Pine Harbor Summer
Evelyn's Pine Harbor Autumn
Lydia's Pine Harbor Christmas

Holiday House

The Christmas Cabin
The Winter Lodge
The Lighthouse
The Christmas Castle
The Beach House
The Christmas Tree Inn
The Holiday Hideaway

Highland Passage

Highland Passage
Knight Errant
Lost Bride

Highland Soldiers

The Enemy
The Betrayal
The Return
The Wanderer

Highland Vow

American Hearts

Secret Hearts
Runaway Hearts
Forbidden Hearts

For more information, visit jljarvis.com.

SNOWSTORM AT CEDAR CREEK

SNOWSTORM AT CEDAR CREEK

J.L. JARVIS

SNOWSTORM AT CEDAR CREEK

Published by Bookbinder Press
bookbinderpress.com

ISBN (paperback) 978-1-942767-44-2
ISBN (ebook) 978-1-942767-43-5

Annie Pope had never thought she was asking for much. From the time she was twelve, she'd had three goals in life—go to college, have a stellar career, and marry Finn Burton. Annie was a practical girl. It wasn't as if Finn was perfect. She'd known him for too long to believe that. But he was perfect for her.

For one thing, his family's summer cottage was next door to hers. While year-round next-door neighbors would have been even better, Annie came to terms with the situation. In fact, she'd decided it was much more romantic because she had all year to remember the previous summer, to wonder what Finn might be doing, how much older he'd look when she saw him again, and whether this would be the summer he'd finally love her back.

If she could go back and talk to her twelve-year-old self, she would tell her it would all turn out just as she'd hoped. She'd be lying, of course, but some things were better left unsaid.

Here she stood, key in hand, at the door to the cottage that had been in her family for three generations. And now, two weeks before Christmas, she was making it her full-time home. Between falling in love with Finn Burton and this moment, thirty years had passed. Spoiler alert—Finn had not fallen in love, at least not with Annie.

She was fine with that now. Still, she looked up at the decades-old horseshoe that hung over the vacation-house door, and she scowled. For years, she had run to the door like she was making a touchdown because her grandmother had told her the first one to pass under the horseshoe got to make a wish. Grandma hadn't exactly lied. She'd just left out the part where the wish wouldn't come true.

At least now Annie knew. This would not be the year Finn loved her back.

Annie soaked in the sight of the familiar stone-and-clapboard cottage that sat beside Cedar Creek, which wound its way through the tall trees. Crisp air stirred the bare branches and tossed about dried leaves. The sight warmed her heart and made her smile. She was home.

When her corporate job shifted to working from home, Annie put her Manlius, New York, house on the market and headed for the family cottage at Cedar Creek in the Adirondack Mountains, her favorite place in the world. With a satisfied sigh, Annie went to her bedroom and, dispensing with formalities, pulled off her bra. She wouldn't see another human until she drove into town for some groceries, so comfort was the rule.

After setting out food and water for her cat, she tugged a sweatshirt over her head and pulled the ends of her mouse-colored shoulder-length hair free. On her way back to the car to unpack, her phone rang. She reflexively glanced at the old rotary-dial wall phone that hung in the kitchen, long since disconnected, and pulled out her cell phone. She smiled when she saw her only child's college graduation photo on the screen. "Hi, Ella. I just walked in the door."

"Good. Mom? Are you busy tonight?"

Annie wrinkled her nose at the odd question. She'd left Ella nearly four hours before, packing boxes in her childhood bedroom. "Uh, let me check my calendar. No." She began a mental list of possible problems. Burst pipes? Tripped circuit breaker?

Maybe just a clogged toilet. Had the realtor called? "Like I said, I just walked in the door. Is everything okay there?"

"Yeah—sorry—everything's fine! I just...uh..."

What's that? Is she suppressing a giggle?

"I... I'll be there in four hours," Ella said. "Don't worry. Everything's fine."

That is a smile. I can hear it in her voice. She is definitely smiling.

"Ella, what's going on? You've got that sound in your voice." Now, that was an absolute giggle, but a secretive one.

"Don't worry," Ella said. "It's all good. See you soon!"

"But—"

"Oh, and Mom?"

"Hold on. You can't just call and—"

"Put on a bra," Ella mumbled, her voice sounding muffled. "Connor's coming with me."

"Connor?" That was a significant item she'd slipped in as if Annie wouldn't notice.

Ella said, "Connor Burton."

Annie rolled her eyes. "I know which Connor."

What I don't know is why Connor Burton—Finn Burton's only child—is with you or why he's coming up here. With my daughter!

Ella laughed. "Gotta go, Mom. See you soon!"

Annie managed, dropped jaw and all, to get out a goodbye. She slipped the phone into her pocket and stared at the wall.

Calm down. Don't jump to conclusions.

There were any number of reasons for Ella to bring Connor here. For instance, they'd gone to the same college, so they'd stayed in touch. That had always seemed so coincidental, the way they'd both wound up at the same school and had run into each other within minutes of arriving at freshmen orientation. But Ella barely spoke about him. To be honest, Ella barely talked to Annie at all anymore. But wasn't that what college was for—to help young people become independent? Four years later, Ella and Connor were still friends—real friends—not like Annie and Finn. Annie had watched for signs that history was repeating itself, but Ella seemed completely happy. In fact, she was far more well-adjusted than Annie had been at her age.

So Connor's there at the house. He was probably just passing through on his way to... somewhere. You're imagining things. Why shouldn't he stop for a visit? Friends do that sort of thing. And, as friends, why wouldn't he and Ella share a ride to the family summer homes? Except then they'll be short a car while they're here.

And then there was Ella's change of plans. She

wasn't supposed to arrive at the cottage for another few days. There was no way she could be finished packing already. Two decades of handmade jewelry, elementary-school dioramas, and God knew what else were crammed into her room—and that wasn't counting whatever was in the closet!

Annie leaned over the kitchen sink and peered through a crack in the blinds. Finn's cottage looked the same as usual. What was not usual was Connor coming here at all. No one but tourists had stayed at that cottage in a year. Vacation renters had come and gone, all overseen by a property manager Annie had run into one day by the mailbox. The property manager had said Finn's A-frame was a popular rental. Annie wasn't surprised. His wife had made sure the place was completely remodeled with a cozy but state-of-the-art kitchen and a modern soaker tub to die for in the bathroom. Gleaming hardwoods and stylish furnishings finished it off. Annie's heart had sunk the first time she'd seen it—not that it wasn't gorgeous. It was. It just didn't look like the cottage she and Finn had run into with red, sweaty faces to gulp glasses of water between childhood adventures.

Annie heaved a sigh. She didn't blame Finn, exactly. Georgina had impeccable taste that was undoubtedly driving renters to stay at their cottage. It was a win-win. Finn was making money renting the cabin, and Annie didn't have to run into him anymore. Or maybe it was the other way around. After all, it had been a full year since she'd seen him. And now Connor was on his way for reasons unknown. She rolled her eyes. Or because his family owned the place. Who wouldn't enjoy parking oneself in an Adirondack chair by the creek, enveloped in the thick scent of pines and the sound of creek water rushing over the rocks?

Annie, you are blowing this out of proportion!

She did that sometimes. She blamed it on living alone. With no one to bounce things off except her cat, Mr. Willoughby, her overactive mind sometimes got the better of her. She took a few deep breaths.

Everything's going to be fine, and if it's not, I will deal with it.

Oh! The car! She'd left the car door open. She rushed outside to unload it. She wasn't worried about theft. Her luggage was more likely to be mauled by a bear than stolen by some passing hiker. It was her car battery she was worried about. She exhaled and got busy. She had a house to air out. And a bra to put on.

Really, Ella?

Three and a half hours later, Annie lit a scented candle, emptied a bag of chips into a bowl, and arranged the cookies on one of her grandmother's plates. The cookies were store-bought, but she hadn't had time to bake. She thought about starting a fire, but she didn't have any logs. Before she had a chance to go outside and check the wood pile, an aggressive knock at the door made her flinch.

Annie turned on the porch light and squinted through the door's beveled-glass window.

"Annie, it's me—Finn."

Annie opened the door and stood staring. "Finn?"

"Hurry, it's freezing out here."

His dark eyes searched hers with an unsettling glint that still made her chest flutter. He gently touched her shoulder to nudge her aside. She stood uselessly by while he rushed in and shut the door behind him. He took off his jacket, hung it on one of the hooks on the wall, and turned, flashing one of those grins that used to make her knees buckle—and still did.

"Finn?" With all the questions racing through her mind, was that the best she could do—a feeble *Finn?*

How about, "Why are you here? Do you know Connor's on his way too? And let's circle back and discuss why you've appeared on my doorstep, and my heart is now pounding like it's 1991."

"We've only got a few minutes. Annie, are you okay? Come here. Let's sit down." He ushered her to a chair at the old kitchen table then got a glass from the cupboard. He knew right where to go. The glasses were in the same place they'd been since Annie and Finn were children.

Annie took a sip of the water he brought her then set the glass down while Finn pulled his chair closer.

"I am so sorry, Annie." Headlights glared through the window. "Oh, crap. I was hoping we'd have time to talk so we'd be on the same page."

Annie's stomach turned over. She wasn't sure why, but Finn obviously knew something she didn't, and she knew him well enough to trust his reaction. She was starting to imagine worst-possible scenarios when Ella walked in with Connor at her heels.

Connor paused, clearly surprised. "Dad?"

"Close the door." Finn's face barely moved except for a slight narrowing of his eyes.

For the first time, Annie sat back and took a good look at him. Finlay Hilderman Burton. The subject of so many wishes and dreams—dreams that had loomed front and center for most of her formative years. Finn looked good—better than good. He wore that salt-and-pepper look well. And his athletic frame had, if anything, gotten fitter. Tiny lines extended from the corners of his dark eyes. But it was that intense gaze of his she remembered the most.

"Mom?"

Absently, Annie glanced at her daughter. *Annie, wake up! You're a terrible mother.* She fixed her eyes on Ella's newly cropped brown hair that didn't quite touch her shoulders. It looked neat and grown-up.

"Mom? Hello. Are you okay?"

Annie attempted a carefree shrug. "Yeah. Yeah, I'm fine." *Is this what a psychotic break feels like?* Her eyes flitted downward but not without seeing the concern on Finn's face.

He reached over and barely touched her shoulder with his fingertips. There went the butterflies—down to her stomach. Then he gave her that look—the same encouraging look he'd given her the first time she'd swung over the creek on the tire swing. It had been more effective when she was seven.

"Why don't we all go sit in the living room?" He said it gently, but it wasn't really a question.

As they all headed out of the kitchen, Connor gently touched Ella's back. *That's different.* Eyes fixed on his hand, Annie froze in her tracks while Ella and Connor walked on ahead.

Finn peered at her. "Annie?"

Finn was always the one to be steady and calm in the face of a crisis. Annie wondered what that must feel like. She resumed her walk to the living room. Ella and Connor had positioned themselves on the sofa, leaving two adjacent armchairs for Annie and Finn.

Connor was a clone of his mother with his dirty-blond hair and Northeast Coast old-money bearing. Annie could still hear Georgina that first summer, whining about how she preferred Newport over the mountains.

"Mom..." Ella's voice trailed off.

Connor put his hand on Ella's and drew in a breath. "Annie..." he said. They were practically family, or used to be, so the kids had always called each other's parents by their first names.

"We're getting married!" Connor announced.

2

Finn stole a sideways glance at Annie. "It's an ongoing discussion."

So Finn knew? Of course he knew. That's what he wanted to tell her.

"Married?" It wasn't as though Annie hadn't guessed. It was near the top of the dozen or so options she'd come up with in the four hours since her daughter had called. "I didn't know you two were dating."

Ella shifted her position on the sofa. "Mom, dating's more of a twentieth-century thing."

Annie caught Finn's eye. His mouth quirked at the corners.

Ignoring her mother's reaction, Ella continued, "We've been friends since freshman year." Connor flashed a surprised look at her. Ella hastened to add, "I mean, not counting here."

Connor said, "Here counts. We've spent every summer together since—forever."

Just as Annie had with Finn. So all of her wishes and dreams had come true but skipped a generation. This was not how it was supposed to work.

Ella said, "My point is, we know each other. Really well. We've been friends for a long time, and since college, we've been more."

Annie lifted an eyebrow.

Connor straightened his posture. "Annie, I've got a good job lined up starting after the holidays. I can support us."

"Support you?" Barely registering Connor's assurance, she turned to her daughter. "What about your career? Or is that more of a twentieth-century thing too?"

Ella leveled a withering stare at her mom. "I'm still looking."

Annie opened her mouth, but no words would come, so she exhaled. She had questions. More than that, she had statements—and a lot of them ended with exclamation points. She needed a minute. "Excuse me."

Annie wrapped her sweater around her and walked out to the porch for some air. The brisk air felt good against her flushed face. Strands of moonlight found their way through pine boughs and shimmered over the water. It was perfect out here—everything she had longed for when she'd made the decision to move. Up to this point, though, her expectations of what her life would be like had blown up. At twenty-one, she had married and, within a year, was a mother and widow. She'd raised Ella alone, pouring all her time and attention into giving her daughter the happiest childhood she could. Not that Annie was a saint. She'd be the first to admit—to herself, anyway—that she'd been hiding. Ella had been her shield from a world that had hurt her. But she'd built a life that was good for them both. If she could fill her daughter with kindness and confidence, Ella would have what she needed to build her own happy life.

Isn't that what she's doing?

It wasn't the concept of marriage that shocked her. It was just so unexpected, and that troubled Annie. Was her daughter about to derail her career and her future, all for Connor? Annie sighed as if she could exhale the ache in her heart. Every parent had dreams for their children, but children had a way of not sticking to the script. Ella was an adult. She was perfectly capable of making decisions—even bad ones. Especially those.

Annie certainly knew about bad decisions. She'd

made one when she was the same age as Ella by—
ironically—eloping with Ella's father. After that, her
life had seemed to unravel along with her career
plans.

Annie wrapped her arms about her waist and
stared at the water.

Behind her, the door gently opened. She glanced
back to see Finn then turned back to the creek.

Finn said, "They're adults. They don't need our
permission."

Annie snapped, "I know that!" She drew in a
deep breath. "Sorry."

"No need to apologize." Same old Finn—quiet
and calm, with a silent strength that once had a young
Annie convinced he was some sort of real-life superhero, her own personal Clark Kent with superpowers
no one but Annie suspected.

She'd spent a lot of time alone reading as a child.

She glanced over at Finn. His Clark Kent glasses
were gone, having disappeared soon after his engagement, no doubt due to corrective eye surgery at
Georgina's insistence. Annie had never minded the
glasses. They'd made him look human. Otherwise, he
was too darned good-looking, with his deep-brown
hair, strong jawline, and gentle hazel eyes. Those eyes
made her weak in the knees. She didn't understand
how he did it, but his gaze didn't just touch her heart

—it held her captive. He was doing it now, and it made her heart ache all over again.

Annie sat down on the porch steps. "Married." If she said it enough, she might begin to accept it. "How did Georgina take the news?"

Finn gazed into the distance with a glint in his eye. "She had other plans for her only child, but she'll come around. How 'bout you?"

Annie lifted her eyebrows and tried to look reassuring. "Finn, please understand, this is not about Connor. I'm just absorbing the shock. But he's your son, so how bad could it be?" She smiled.

His eyes crinkled. "Relax. He's a way better version of me."

Annie tried to seem duly amused. The guy had no idea how much he'd hurt her. He'd never done it on purpose, but that almost made it worse. She couldn't even hate him.

Finn's smile faded. "The thing is, I honestly think they're in love."

"And that's all they need, isn't it?" She smiled, but she knew how bitter she sounded. She shook off the emotion.

Their eyes met and darted away. From inside the rustling trees, birds sang. Lovebirds. Perfect.

"Some marriages are happy." Finn broke the silence.

"So I hear." Annie took a quiet breath. *Don't do this.* "I'm sorry. It just seems so rushed."

"Only because we didn't know about it. Knowing Connor, he's compiled a spreadsheet with contingency tables."

"Ella never told me a thing."

Finn's easy smile annoyed her. "Come on, Annie. Did you tell your parents about every guy in your life?"

She frowned. "Well, not every guy, only the serious ones."

"What about me? What did you tell them?"

Is he smiling? No, he is laughing at me. I can't decide whether he's a fool or a jerk.

She smirked. "About you? They knew all they needed to know."

That drew a robust laugh. The last thing she felt like doing was smiling, but she did. She'd had so many years of practice at playing along, as if her heart didn't throb when his eyes settled on hers.

A warm smile lit his eyes. "I've always loved that about you."

"What?" *Please stop staring at me.* She tried to look annoyed.

"You're just Annie."

How many years had she forced this same smile? "Thanks."

"No, I mean it."

Just Annie. I get it, so please stop insisting. This is not going to be about me. My daughter is in there making the biggest choice—or mistake—of her life. I need to do something. A sudden thought came to her like a punch in the gut. She stared at Finn. "I'm an idiot."

Before he could react, she went inside and confronted her daughter.

"You're pregnant." She shot a look at Connor, whose jaw dropped as he shook his head no. "I can't believe it took me this long to figure it out."

Ella leapt to her feet. "Mom! Oh my gosh! Get a grip! I'm not pregnant!"

Annie followed Ella's indignant gaze to the doorway, where Finn stood as though planning a hasty retreat. At that moment, he looked like anything but a superhero as he wore a confused frown. Connor had a deer-in-the-headlights expression. With an eye roll, Ella heaved a huge sigh, no doubt realizing she was on her own. Everyone around her was engulfed in their own individual torment.

"Mom, people get married all the time—people who aren't even pregnant!" Ella cried. "Sometimes, they're just in love! Not that you'd know anything about that."

Annie felt as though the wind had been knocked

out of her, and then she felt sick to her stomach. In fact, Annie did know all about love and how much it could hurt.

Her daughter dissolved into tears. "Thanks for trusting me, Mom!" With that, she rushed outside through the kitchen door, followed closely by Connor.

Finn walked into the kitchen and glanced toward the screen door. "That went well."

Annie rolled her eyes. "Yeah. I'm having a really great day." She went into the living room and sank onto the sofa.

A short time later, Finn came from the kitchen with two beers.

Annie frowned at the beers. "So are you, I see."

Finn smiled. "One's for you."

She took it. "I don't drink beer."

"I know. But I thought you might make an exception for the occasion."

Annie lifted her eyes to meet his then took the beer and downed half of it. With a grimace, she wiped her mouth. "Blegh! I don't know how college kids do this." Then she belched spectacularly, and he laughed.

How can he laugh at a time like this?

"I'm impressed." He sat down beside her and

stretched out his legs, resting his feet on the coffee table. He leaned back his head as Annie had done, and the two of them stared at the ceiling. A memory warmed Annie's heart. Finn was repeating a childhood ritual. After long morning swims, they'd plop down on a sofa in one of their houses and wait for the inevitable PB&Js to arrive from whichever parent was closest to the kitchen. As he had so many times before, Finn said, "I spy with my little eye something that is blue."

Annie turned to face his knowing look. "Me?"

Kindness shone in his eyes.

A wave of sadness washed over her. "They grew up."

"Dang kids."

That coaxed a smile from her.

"Is it really so bad?" He leaned closer. *Oh man, he smells good.*

She frowned and reluctantly answered him. "No."

"They're adults."

"Young adults."

Something about his amused reaction annoyed her.

Finn asked, "How old were you when you first fell in love?"

He'd just touched a nerve, and he had no idea.

The answer was twelve, but she sure wasn't going to tell him.

He leaned away, studying her. "Now, that is a very intriguing expression. Is there something you haven't told me?"

"You're an idiot."

A broad smile lit his face. "No, you've told me that numerous times."

She smiled and wistfully said, "Yeah, I have, haven't I?"

"Look, they're young, but still... they're twenty-one. We'd have a pretty hard time stopping the wedding."

Annie exhaled. "Why is it you can get married younger than you can rent a car?"

Finn leveled that look that always meant he couldn't be bothered to argue the point. "Look, Connor has a great job lined up." Annie drew in a breath, but Finn cut her off. "And Ella will find a job too."

Annie didn't realize she was shaking her head until Finn told her not to.

"Come on, Annie." He nudged her shoulder with his like he used to when they were kids. "It's not like they just met. They used to play in a wading pool together."

"I should never have let her bathe topless." She smiled begrudgingly.

"They've spent four years in college together. They're smart. They're in love. They'll be fine."

"I know. It's just kind of a shock." A tear appeared out of nowhere and clouded her vision. She wiped it away before Finn could notice. Or maybe he did.

He teasingly leaned against her shoulder again. "Come on, Oakley."

That did it. He knew how that nickname annoyed her. She whipped her head toward him. But instead of the smirk she'd expected, his eyes softened, dissolving her annoyance.

Gently, he said, "You looked like you needed a laugh." But she wasn't laughing, and neither was he. He was staring into her eyes, and she was drowning in his gaze. Guys with soft hazel eyes had a duty to take care whom they looked at like that. Not everyone could handle that sort of rapt attention.

Finn said, "They're in love."

Annie set down her beer and winced. "I hope so."

She turned to Finn. Maybe he did have superpowers, because his gaze overpowered her panic and calmed her—so much so that she let down her guard. "I just wasn't prepared to let go." She fought to tamp down her emotions.

Finn touched her hand, then he gave it a squeeze. "I know. But maybe it's time." He let go.

Annie searched his eyes. "Is that what you're doing? You're just letting go?"

He shrugged. "What choice do I have?"

Annie tried but couldn't come up with an answer.

Finn leaned his elbows on his knees and stared off to the distance. He turned long enough for a knowing glance back, and a twinkle came into his eyes. "On the bright side, we'll be family." He grinned.

She'd once dreamed about being a family together, but never like this. She made a serious effort to smile.

Finn asked, "What do you say we go find them and give them our blessing?"

3

Finn followed Annie to the driveway. She was right. Ella and Connor were young. So was he when he'd fallen for Annie. He'd been backpacking through Europe with his college girlfriend, Tamara. But when they got off the train at Amsterdam Central station, they parted ways.

She said she was tired of youth hostels and even more tired of him. Then she kissed him on the cheek. "There's my train." She smiled and walked away.

He spent a week wandering the streets alongside the canals in a daze, his thoughts only interrupted by tingling handlebar bells as the occasional bicyclist swerved to miss him. It was then that he grew to appreciate the impressive grasp the Dutch had on English—especially curse words. Halfway through the Hermitage Museum, with tales of

Napoleon and Josephine clouding his mind—or maybe it was the wafting weed smoke he'd walked through on the way—he had an epiphany. What if Annie was his Josephine, the one constant love of his life?

He still didn't know where the thought came from, but the idea stuck. He'd caught the next train to Schiphol Airport and headed for home. Not even a middle seat on the long flight home could quell his new joy. Annie Pope. Why hadn't he seen it before?

With merciful timing, Annie glanced at him over her shoulder and drew him back to the present. He didn't need to relive what had come next. So he shook off the memories and followed Annie to their two kids who were crazy in love. He couldn't help but notice from his current perspective that Annie had held up pretty well over the years.

From a few steps away, Annie said, "Ella—"

"Mom, it's okay." From the way she regarded her mother, it clearly was not. "I mean, it's not, but I want... can't you just be happy for us?"

Finn glanced at Connor. They'd survived the explosion. Now they just had to contend with the fallout. Connor held Ella's hand so securely that if she fell off a cliff, she'd be safe, but her fingers might turn blue from the lost circulation.

Given how Annie had reacted to the news, she looked surprisingly stoic. Anyone watching her might have thought she was taking the news in stride, but Finn knew her. Annie grew quiet when she was upset. From the way Ella shifted her weight back and forth, she seemed to pick up on Annie's tension.

Annie whispered, "I'm sorry. I was shocked. I just didn't expect it."

Ella stared downward, jaw clenched.

Annie tenderly lifted Ella's chin. "Are you happy?"

Through her tears, Ella said, "Yes."

Annie turned to Connor. "What have you got to say for yourself?"

Connor looked straight at Annie. "I love her."

"Good answer." Annie didn't move for a moment. "Okay. But if you ever hurt her, I'll—"

"You'll have to get in line behind me." Finn took a step forward and stood beside Annie.

Annie smiled, truly smiled, for the first time, and it lit up her face—his as well. He remembered a time when she used to smile all the time. It was so long ago. Before he lost himself in her gaze, Finn stretched out his arms. "Bring it in. Let's have a group hug so we can go in and break open a bottle of—something!"

They all laughed and hugged before heading back inside together.

Annie opened and closed cupboards, looking for something to toast with. Finn headed for the door. "Before you reach for the vanilla extract, let me run next door. I'm sure I've got something appropriate."

Outside, the night sounds weren't nearly as loud as his thoughts. He wasn't any more thrilled than Annie about the engagement. Connor and Ella would barely have time to be adults on their own before taking on the challenges a marriage could bring. But Finn wasn't too old to remember being Connor's age and in love. That memory was the root cause of his apprehension. He had followed his heart to Europe, gotten dumped there, then suddenly discovered his feelings for Annie. He'd never had a chance to explore what those feelings were. Feelings ran a broad spectrum. He just knew they were deep.

Finn paused with a bottle of wine in his hand. *What if?* The question had haunted him over the years.

You can't build a life with what-ifs. But it would have been a much happier life.

Finn paused at Annie's door, drew in a breath, and walked inside with a bright-eyed expression. He grabbed four glasses and poured. "Here's to love and a lifetime of happiness!"

Although they all gave the appearance of ease, there were subtle signs of strain between Annie and Ella. They were pleasant, even cheerful, but Annie had a habit that had always betrayed her. Since they were kids, she'd always smoothed her hair back from her forehead—even if there was none there. She'd lift her eyebrows as if she were trying to convince herself everything was fine. At the moment, she was convincingly forcing a smile. She was good. But a few glances between her daughter and Connor made it clear Ella wasn't buying any of it.

Hours later, after reminiscing about past summers together and Connor and Ella's PG version of how their college years had brought them to this point, Annie stifled a yawn.

"Are we boring you, Mother?" Ella grinned, but it didn't reach her eyes.

Finn came to the rescue. "It is after midnight."

Connor shifted his weight as though he were about to get up. Then he looked at Ella. "I hadn't planned this far ahead, but of course, we'll have to stay over."

Ella's eyes locked on Connor's.

Finn studied Annie. She appeared composed until she lifted her eyebrows. He guessed what she was thinking. She'd barely had time to adjust—she couldn't be expected to host a sleepover. Cheerily, Finn said, "Connor, the loft in the A-frame is just as you left it. Well, a little cleaner, but you get the idea." He gave Connor his Dad look to make sure he got the idea.

It took Annie a few seconds to catch on. She turned to Ella. "There are clean sheets and towels in the linen closet."

Ella was silent and expressionless for long moments. "Okay," she finally said.

Finn clapped his hands on his knees and got up. "It's been..." *No, "long day" wouldn't sound right. "Eventful day" sounds snarky.* "An exciting evening." *Right.* Not exactly the first thought anyone here would have looking back on this evening, but "shocking" would have been worse. He started to smile but caught Connor's look. Since his son was age ten, that expression had meant only one thing: *What is your problem?*

Finn slept surprisingly well. Some things were inevitable. Anything adult children did fell under that umbrella. His son was a grown man, and he'd made a choice. To Connor's credit, he'd made a far better choice than Finn had at his age. Maybe that was why Finn had taken the news better than Annie. Ella wasn't perfect, but he couldn't imagine her making anyone miserable—not like Finn had been with Georgina. Finn had married a beautiful woman. That made Finn an idiot, because he thought that was enough. What was worse, she had a brain, and she knew how to use it. But he'd made a commitment, so he hung in there for years. Of course, the wedding vows were enough of a reason to stick around, but when he talked her out of an abortion, he had an even stronger reason. He'd vowed to be there for Connor— and he always was.

Be happy, Connor.

Finn was still lazily lounging in bed when a loud and relentless knocking sounded on his front door. *Wow, Ella's eager.* He hollered, "Connor! Can you get the door?"

Silence.

"Connor?" Finn exhaled and begrudgingly dragged himself out of bed. He grabbed the jeans he'd left draped on a chair, pulled them on, glanced about, found a T-shirt, went to the door, and opened it. "Annie?"

She stormed in and plopped down in a chair at

the kitchen island. "Unbelievable!" She shook her head for a moment, lifted red-rimmed eyes, and scowled. "You look awfully calm."

Finn squinted. "I just got up. I can't think before coffee. You know that. But I'm not really calm. This is more of a coma."

She cast him a scathing glare then shook her head and grabbed his grandmother's coffee canister but stopped when she saw a note taped to it. Without so much as a glance to see what the note said, she pulled it off the canister and handed it to Finn. "Oh, look." She sounded unsurprised. "You got one too."

By the time Finn finished reading, he heard coffee dripping in the pot. "They've got to be kidding."

Annie nodded. "What does it say?"

Finn read, "'We're going to Vegas. We'll be back at my apartment in time for my first day of work.'"

"Mine says, 'I'm sorry. I know you're not happy about our engagement. Preparing for a wedding would be worse—and expensive, so we've eloped.'"

Finn and Annie stared at each other in stunned silence. Someone had to say something. The tension was too thick to bear. "Think of the money you're saving." He smiled, hoping she'd see the bright side or at least laugh.

Annie narrowed her eyes. "Drink your coffee." She left.

What did I say? Finn followed her as far as the door and pondered the question until she got back to her cottage.

4

Annie sat in the kitchen and exhaled. She'd been abrupt if not rude. Finn didn't deserve that. She was angry but not at him. She wasn't even sure whom she was angry with. Connor and Ella were just being kids, except that they weren't. They were adults, and they were in love. Still, Annie had every right to be taken aback by her daughter's sudden decision to run off and get married, but couples did that all the time. Actually, what they did even more often was skip the wedding and move in together. She ought to be happy they'd gone the traditional route, but she couldn't help her knee-jerk reaction. Worse, she couldn't understand it.

And then there was Finn, someone she'd relegated to a wave from across the figurative fence she'd erected between them. To be fair, he'd tried to smooth over the tension. That was Finn in a nutshell. No matter how many years passed since the days they were close, she could go to him if she needed to. She never did, but knowing she could made life's dark moments manageable. She hadn't been fair to him by walking away with no explanation. He probably knew she didn't blame him for Ella and Connor running away to elope, but he deserved to be told that.

Annie followed the creek to a canopied place in the woods where the sun shone through a bare patch in the overhead branches, casting a warm amber glow. She'd found the secret clearing during a childhood adventure and returned to it whenever she needed time alone. She sat down on a bench she had fashioned from logs, and she breathed in the earthy scent of the creek bank as the water gurgled by. Even after all these years, this was the one place that made her feel in control.

That was the crux of her problem. She'd lost control. When her marriage with Matt had been spinning out of control, Annie had never let her troubles show in other parts of her life. That was a fact she was proud of. Matt had broken her heart long before he'd left her.

Left you. Can't you admit it yet? Matt didn't leave you. He died.

There went her self-control. Ignoring the tears that moistened her eyes, she was still. It was only a wave of grief. It would pass. After twenty-one years, she'd learned to give in to the waves. They always passed, and life went on again. But for those moments, she felt the same desperate loss of control.

That was why she had walked away from Finn earlier. She had to. She couldn't let him see her like that. She'd spent too many years maintaining her grace-under-pressure facade to let it tumble down in a heap in one weak moment.

As a rule, she tried not to care what people thought, but the looks on their faces weren't always easy to bear. That sort of pity felt like a knife to the heart, even though it often came from genuine kindness. Seeing a similar expression in Finn's eyes would destroy her.

Her life was okay. It was good. She had made it that way. She had been twenty-one when she lost her husband. Lost. As if she'd misplaced him. No one lost Matt. He'd been bigger than life but not bigger than the tree he wrapped his car around. His death came as a shock to everyone except Annie. When she met him, his burning passion for life had thrilled her. He appeared like a flash of brilliant light, as though he'd been sent to deliver her from her love for Finn. And it worked. He was the antidote, the polar opposite of Finn in every way. After years of pining away over Finn, she could finally let go and leave him behind. Matt swept her away with his burning intensity. He adored her, at least for a few months. If only she'd known his devotion that exploded like fireworks lighting the sky would burn out as quickly.

Before long, Matt had moved onto his next adrenaline high. His addiction was danger. If it was risky, he did it—cliff jumping, paragliding, zip lining, skydiving, and rock climbing. There was no limit to what he would try. But his life was all about the next thrill, and Annie wasn't it anymore. As far as she knew, he was faithful to her, but he'd lost interest. He was overjoyed about having a baby. But by then, Annie felt out of the loop in her own marriage.

When she went into labor, she called him, but he didn't answer. She texted and got no response. By the time she'd given birth to Ella, she was a widow. For all of Matt's dangerous sports, he'd died in a car wreck on the way to work.

She angrily brushed away tears. *Annie, what are you doing?* She finally got it. She wasn't crying for Matt or even for Ella. She was crying for herself, for the time she had lost. The white-knuckled grip she'd kept on her life and Ella's had been an absurd lie—most of all to herself. Life happened the way it was going to happen. For all of her love, she couldn't protect Ella from learning that lesson the hard way.

"I thought I'd find you here."

"Finn!" As if her startled expression didn't tell him as much, she added, "You scared me!"

He settled beside her in his usual place. "Sorry. I thought you'd hear me coming."

She shook her head no. "That's okay."

Birdsong and rustling leaves were the only sounds until Finn drew in a breath. But before he could speak, Annie said, "Finn, I'm sorry. I wasn't angry with you."

Unsurprised, he said, "I know. You're too busy beating yourself up to be angry with me."

She shot him a sharp look. But the truth of his words sank in. He was on the right track, of course. This was Finn. If anyone got her, he did. "I just wanted to spare Ella what I think is a—" Abruptly, she stopped and began again. "A hasty decision."

"I don't know. Connor tells me they've been together for four years."

"Well, I know Ella." *She's got romantic ideas like I did when I was her age.* Annie could feel his eyes on her.

"Annie, they'll be okay." She flashed him a doubtful look, but he continued. "And if they're not, they're adults now. They'll figure it out."

"Maybe they will, but I won't." She flitted her eyes toward him. "I forgot how annoying it is when you're right."

He grinned. "I'm still right all the time. You just haven't been around to see it."

That irked her, although she didn't quite know why. "I'm around all the time—well, at least every summer. So are you."

He smirked, and it felt like they'd picked up where they'd left off years ago. "Well, I guess—if you can count waving from the driveway while you're bringing in your groceries or walking out to the car."

Because I'm my best around you at arm's length. A driveway's length is even better. "It's been a busy few years—decades, really."

Finn's expression softened.

Could he see what that did to her? It felt so obvious to her—her flushed cheeks, throbbing pulse, and helplessness to control it.

He said, "Maybe it's for the best—the marriage. Now you'll have some time to yourself."

He was trying to cheer her up. She wanted to convince him that he'd succeeded, but her heart contracted, and her emotions took over. "You're right. I will."

"That's a good thing, isn't it?" He seemed sincerely confused.

She forced a confident nod. "Yes."

His eyes softened. "Annie. I'm here if you need me. And you've always got Mr. Willoughby."

That drew a smile. "He does adore me."

"He's not the only one."

Of course, he meant it in a platonic way, but his unwavering gaze made her heart skip a beat. Thanks to years of practice, she managed to hold it together. "When Ella went to college, the hardest part was the holidays. She was home for the big ones, but the little ones, when I had the day off, sometimes felt long."

"It just so happens that I've a little extra time on my hands these days. So if you feel like reliving the old days, just let me know."

That familiar inner glow flared up. That was such a Finn thing to say. "Thanks." A sudden thought gripped her heart. "I forgot about Christmas."

His eyes twinkled. "December twenty-fifth. Every year."

Annie smirked. He was trying to lighten her mood, but it couldn't help this time. "I mean I forgot that Ella might not be able to come home for Christmas."

Finn drew in air through clenched teeth. "Georgina's family does have their big Christmas ski thing every year. But she can't expect Connor to spend every Christmas with her. They'll have to work that out. But what if you and I shared? If you're will-ing, Connor and Ella could spend every other Christmas with us."

Annie wasn't following him. "But why wouldn't you be with Georgina?"

His face went blank. "Oh. You don't know. Because I haven't told you. We're divorced."

She hoped her face didn't display all the emotions running through her. When she recovered from the shock, she said, "I didn't know."

"I should have mentioned it sooner. It's been six months. I ought to be used to it, but I keep forgetting who knows and who doesn't, and I hate having to talk about it."

"Finn, I'm sorry."

He shook his head. "Things were bad for so long that by the time she left me, she was putting me out of my misery. But still... when it happened, it was some-thing to deal with."

Annie didn't know what to say. She hadn't known? But he knew that already. What else was there to say—that she was sorry? That she never liked Georgina? That she had no idea? But that wasn't true. She'd kept her distance over the years, but even from next door, she'd noticed he only appeared happy when he was with Connor. She could envision them even now, walking down to the creek with their fishing gear or playing catch in the yard.

Her silence seemed to prompt him to explain. "I know. After two decades of marriage, you're wondering what took us so long."

Annie shook her head, but she did, in fact, wonder.

He glanced at her. "This is going to sound... I don't know. I just believe they're called wedding vows for a reason. And there was Connor. Anyway, the short version is, I hung in there. By the time Connor left for college, Georgina and I were in the same house but living two separate lives."

Annie was too stunned to speak. They'd spent years doing no more than waving and saying hello from their driveways. Now here he was, opening up. It was a lot to take in.

He let out a bitter laugh under his breath. "I don't know why it should matter, but it really pissed me off that she left me for some guy in her spin class."

Annie winced.

Finn nodded. "I know. After twenty-two years of marriage." He shook his head. "Man, I'm old. So are you." A grin bloomed on his face as he looked sideways at her.

Annie gave his shoulder a shove. "Thanks."

"Sorry, Oakley. Can I help it if I'm good at math?"

"Same old Finn. And by that, I mean same *really old* Finn." She narrowed her eyes, but inside, she was smiling. For a moment, it felt as though they'd time-traveled back to their teens.

"Look at us now. Right back where we started." Finn's smile faded as he gazed into the distance.

She knew he didn't mean anything by it, but she felt disappointed. Back then, she had so much hope for her future. It hadn't turned out at all like she'd thought it would.

Finn seemed completely at ease as he rested his elbows on his knees, lost in thought. "How did you do it?"

She wasn't sure what he meant, so she waited.

"Wasn't it hard being alone all those years?"

His word stung just a little. "I wasn't alone. I had Ella. You know, kids keep you busy."

He looked at her as though he could see straight through to the truth she was hiding.

Annie averted her eyes. "Well, I would have preferred being blissfully in love, living happily ever after, but I wasn't. In love, I mean. I wasn't desperately lonely, if that's what you're worried about. I'd much rather be alone than with the wrong person."

He flinched. It was slight but enough for her to

get a good read on his thoughts. Her words had struck a nerve, which she hadn't intended. "Finn, I was talking about myself. I didn't mean... anything."

A soft smile lit his eyes. "Annie, relax. I know what you meant. I also know that you're right. It was like having chronic pain—being with the wrong person." He smiled then drew in a deep breath and exhaled. "What were we thinking? A New York cop and a fashion designer? Anyway, now I'm divorced. It's not like we were happily married, but it caught me off guard. It's all good. I'm making it work. This is my happy ending."

Annie didn't feel happy at all for either of them.

Finn wrinkled his face as he thought for a moment. "I've kind of been dreading Christmas. It's my first one alone. All those happy shoppers bustling around with their shopping bags and lattes might just make me puke." He laughed.

An image flashed into Annie's mind and brought back a memory. "Couples in candlelit restaurant windows... that used to get to me sometimes."

He nodded.

She added, "But I had the good taste not to press my nose to the window glass by their tables."

He nodded approvingly. "Classy choice."

"I thought so."

He narrowed his eyes as if mulling over an idea.

"If the kids both go to Georgina's, we'll both be alone."

"Yeah."

"So... we could do Christmas together."

His words took her by surprise. "Well, I suppose it depends on what Ella and Connor decide."

"I'm not just talking Christmas day. Think about it. I mean, we're friends. What are friends for? We could do Christmas things together. We could be that disgusting couple in the restaurant window. Or those annoying shoppers happily bustling about with their shopping bags! But I draw the line at lattes."

His infectious enthusiasm warmed Annie. "What are your views on hot chocolate? Because that would be a deal breaker for me."

"Oh, chocolate is essential!"

With a growing smile, Annie said, "Good. I think we can hammer out an agreement."

The light, friendly moment slowly shifted into something more serious as they gazed at each other. Finn broke the silence with a quiet, "I'm glad."

Annie told herself it made sense. They'd catch up and get through what could otherwise be a difficult time.

Finn's face brightened. "If the newlyweds show up for Christmas, we can all spend it together. And if

Georgina guilts them into going to her, we'll still have each other."

Annie felt a twinge of excitement as she anticipated the next two weeks leading up to Christmas with Finn. "I've got some vacation time coming."

"I was wondering if you worked. I'm not sure I've seen you leave the house except for groceries."

She smirked. "Oh, I work. I just work from home as an insurance biller. But I'm about to take two weeks off. So there!"

Finn seemed pleased. "While we're brokering this deal, we should include a clause to give you an out in case I get on your nerves."

Annie tried to look serious. "I was worried about that."

"Who could blame you?"

"We could do it like an apartment lease, but instead of month to month, we could take it day to day."

He extended his hand to seal the deal with a handshake. "I can live with that."

Annie shook his hand. "Well, I guess it's a plan." Unexpected joy filled Annie, so bright that she tried to suppress it in case she seemed overly pleased to the point of weirdness. It was only a couple of weeks between friends.

With an emphatic nod, Finn stood. Annie

followed his lead. As they headed back to their homes, Finn's eyes sparkled. "I can't wait to see you in a Santa suit, Oakley."

She looked at him wryly. "Only if you dress as an elf."

5

Fishing made everything better. The fresh, bracing air, the scent of the mossy creek banks, and the sound of the water tripping over the rocks was all it took to clear Finn's head and soothe his senses. There was nothing in life he couldn't overcome with a rod, reel, and fly line. Fishing had gotten him through his divorce, not to mention the marriage that led up to it. And before that? Well, the list was too long. He had made many mistakes in his life.

It all started with Annie. There were constants in life, not just the constants that anchor a person like family, home, and career. Those were the typical foundational pillars, but Finn was convinced everyone had something or someone that guided their thoughts and decisions. Deeper than a hobby or passion, it was an underlying presence that centered a person. For Finn, it had always been Annie. In some ways, she was everything he was not. Even as children, no matter the adventure, it had always been better with Annie. She was like a prism that made everything appear better. At some point in his life that he couldn't pinpoint, he'd unexpectedly found himself wishing she were with him so he could see things through her eyes. Maybe if he'd told her about that, he might not have lost her.

Most young people find college to be a transformative signpost in their lives when they become independent and productive adults. In Finn's case, it was a chance to be stupid, and he'd excelled at it. By anyone's measure, he had never been an astute intellectual. It wasn't that he couldn't have managed the schoolwork. He just didn't care. So once he'd done enough to get by, he had time on his hands. In the history of college students, no student ever had trouble filling free time. Spending hours in a library study carrel worked for some but not Finn. He was the happiest outdoors and found an on-campus alternative to his usual hiking and fishing. By accident, he discovered that his favorite college pastime, idly strumming his guitar, was a chick magnet. If he planted himself on the quad, ladies appeared. Adding a dog would have been even better. At least that was his theory. But dogs weren't allowed in the dorms, so he'd never had the chance to put it to the test.

The fish weren't biting, so Finn spied a better spot and got settled there. Morning sun filtered through the thick tree branches and mottled the banks of the creek. Bits of sun danced in flecks on the water, while birds chattered unseen in the trees. Just past the bend in the creek hung a knotted rope from a large over-hanging bough that leaned over a deep stretch of water. He could almost see Annie swinging from the banks to the middle of the creek and letting go. Then he would follow. Back then, they must have spent hours there, taking occasional breaks to lie on a sunny patch of grass a few yards from the water. There, they would stretch out on their backs and look up at the clouds and make up stories to go with what they saw.

Looking back, he could see there were moments that could have led to a different kind of relationship. Their eyes would meet and linger until someone averted their gaze. Innocent touches, such as a stray hand that happened to brush the other person or shoulders that touched as they strolled side by side, became awkward. After a while, there were no more moments. Almost as if they'd formed an unspoken pact, they walked a bit farther apart, grew a little less playful, and lost the unselfconscious spontaneity they'd once shared. In short, things had changed, and they'd gone to college.

Slow learner that he apparently was, it took Finn four years of college to figure out what he wanted. After graduation, Tamara Barnhill, his girlfriend of four months, had suggested they backpack through Europe. He could think of no more breathtaking a way to avoid working at the local grocery store for yet another summer, so he agreed. Upon close examination, he came up short on funds. His modest savings and graduation gifts wouldn't get him far, but Tamara had a trust fund. She had to stay somewhere, so bringing him along wouldn't cost her any more. So they booked a cheap flight and, armed with their passports and a youth hostel directory, they headed for Europe.

A few weeks into the trip, they were in Paris. As they walked alongside the bookstalls lining the Seine, he picked up an old edition of *The Secret Garden*. He could see nine-year-old Annie curled up in a hammock, reading it. He'd called her boring and snatched it from her hands. She was a good reader and an even better fighter. That afternoon, Annie finished her book while he held a bag of frozen mixed vegetables to his blackening eye.

Book in hand, Finn turned to Tamara and asked if she'd ever read it.

She shrugged. "I was never much of a reader." Her face brightened. "And now that we're finished with college, I don't have to be." She turned away, missing his baffled reaction, then said, "Let's go window shop on the Champs-Élysées.

That was when he realized Tamara wasn't Annie. He tried to shake off the thought, but he found himself at the most inopportune moments imagining how much better it would be if Annie were there. Evidently, Tamara was more intuitive than he'd thought. The day they left Paris for Amsterdam, she informed him it wasn't working out between them. When they got to Amsterdam, she'd be going on solo.

There he stood in the Gare du Nord, coffee and croissant in hand. "You're breaking up with me?"

"Nothing personal. We're just parting ways." She wrapped her arms around his neck. "It's been fun."

"Yeah." He wasn't sure whether he was more confused or relieved.

Relieved. Finn sat on a bench and ate his croissant. A week later, his plane touched down at JFK. In Amsterdam, he'd worked it all out. He loved Annie. It was so obvious, but he had been too close to Annie for too long to recognize what it was. He was in love.

Desperate to see Annie, he caught a train from Penn Station to the mountains and got off at Westport, the station closest to Cedar Creek, where his worried mother was waiting in the car.

"Nothing's wrong," he explained. "Tamara and I parted ways, and I decided it was time to come home. Can we stop at the store? I need to pick up some... deodorant." *Deodorant?* It was all he could think of. What he wanted to do was see Annie. For some reason, he was sure she'd be working a shift at the local food market. The two of them had always worked late on Friday afternoons. Tourists were arriving in town and stocking up for the weekend, and the locals were getting off work. It was always busy and staffed up accordingly.

Fifteen minutes later, Finn walked out of the store with a stick of deodorant he didn't need. Annie didn't work there anymore. When Finn left for Europe, Annie had planned to work there for the summer and apply for jobs in her spare time. He could only assume she'd found a job early on, which was great. She'd worked hard all through college and deserved all the success that would inevitably come her way. In the meantime, he couldn't wait to see her.

It wasn't until they got home and he headed out

the door that his mother said, "If you're going to see Annie, she's gone."

He hung his jacket on a hook by the door and paused, feeling grim. "What?" He already knew he did not want to know the details.

"Annie's..." Her voice trailed off.

"What?" By this time, he was sure Annie had either died or joined the Peace Corps.

"She's married."

Looking helpless, his mother lifted her shoulders. "I'm not sure what else to tell you. His name's Matt. He came up from the city. Annie's mom said they met at the store. He's got money. I don't know what to say. He swept her off her feet, and one day, they drove off and got married."

"Annie would have told me."

"She didn't tell anyone until after the fact."

"Married?" He'd shaken his head slowly and softly said, "Wow." Realizing his mother was studying him, he'd said, "I'm going to go for a walk."

Here he was, fishing in the same place he'd fished over the years. It was his go-to place when he needed a break from his life. This was where he'd gone when the tension in his marriage had weighed heavily on him, and when tension had evolved to apathy, he'd come here even more. This was the one place he felt balanced. He laughed to himself. That meant he was unbalanced the rest of the time.

He wasn't catching anything, so he packed up his fishing gear and paused for a minute to take in the sight. The trees had grown taller. So had Finn. But one thing hadn't changed. He still loved Annie.

After he put away his gear, he walked inside and pulled out a beer from the otherwise empty fridge. Someone knocked at the door. He didn't get many visitors here, which was one of his favorite things about the cabin.

He swung open the door. "Annie." Realizing he was a little too happy to see her, he tried to look whatever cool looked like at age forty-three.

She held out a brown paper package.

With a grin, he said, "You shouldn't have. It's not even my birthday."

She gave him a tolerant smile. "They left this on my doorstep."

He took it and beckoned her inside. "Come on in. I was just having a beer, and I shouldn't drink alone."

He forged on to the kitchen despite not hearing her footsteps behind him. By the time he turned, she'd joined him. Before she changed her mind, he pulled out a beer and handed it to her. As he did, he wondered if it would be too obvious if, for future deliveries, he changed his house number to hers. *Yeah, she'd see through that.* The thought amused him, though.

"Why are you smiling?" She seemed suspicious.

"Huh?" He shrugged, which he realized looked more awkward than nonchalant. "Oh, 'cause it's nice to see you."

Her eyebrows drew together. "You saw me this morning."

"It's always nice to see you." That was the absolute truth.

Annie's smirky scowl hadn't changed much over the years. He laughed. "That's the face. That's my Annie."

A flicker of an emotion he couldn't quite pinpoint lit her eyes for an instant, and then it was gone. Eager to get past the uneasy silence, Finn said, "I was just about to order a pizza. Do you still like pepperoni?"

She seemed a little surprised. "Uh, yeah."

Before she could add a "but," he said, "Good." He picked up his phone and placed the order. "Thirty minutes." His eyes twinkled.

Annie stared knowingly. "Has it ever been thirty minutes?"

"No. Come on. Let's go sit down." They sat on a

sofa that faced a wall of windows looking out at the creek. "You didn't have big plans tonight, did you?"

"No, you caught me on my one free night of the week."

He couldn't tell if she was serious, which must have shown on his face.

"I'm kidding. I spent so much time driving Ella around that I've become kind of a recluse since she went to college."

"Nothing wrong with that."

"I guess not."

"Although, I remember a time when your life was a social whirlwind."

A slight blush came to her cheeks, and her eyes clouded over. "That was Matt. I just went along for the ride."

Finn wanted to kick himself. "Annie, I'm sorry. I didn't mean to bring up..."

She peered at him with a searching expression that made him wonder what she wanted to say, but she held back. He wished she would trust him. But they'd barely spoken for years, at least not about serious things. How could he expect her to just open up now?

Annie said, "It was a long time ago."

It was all Finn could do not to ask all the questions he'd wondered about, the main one being why.

Why had she married a man so unsuited to her personality? She had so much more to offer, and she'd deserved more than he'd given her. He'd seen her reading on the screened-in back porch in the evenings. Always alone. People sat outside alone, but with her, it was different. He knew what it felt like to be that alone in a marriage because he'd felt it too.

Annie's eyes brightened. "Board games!"

"What?" Unprepared, he quickly shifted gears to catch up with her. Annie went to the built-in wall of shelves and retrieved a falling-apart box of Scrabble. "How many rainy days did we spend playing board games?"

"More than I wanted to, because you always kicked my butt."

"Yeah, I did, didn't I?" She set free the smile she'd been suppressing. "Sorry."

"I can tell."

Annie gazed at the game box then lifted her eyes to meet Finn's. "Wanna play?"

Two hours later, Finn leaned back and stretched while Annie cheerily slid the game tiles back into the box. "I don't know why I let you do that to me again," he said.

"Because it's fun?"

Finn balked. "For you, maybe!"

"Oh, right. Because you can't take it that there's

one thing—one single, solitary thing—I do better than you?"

He put on a wounded expression. "I can take it. I just don't enjoy it."

She burst into laughter. "Boo hoo, poor you!"

Their eyes met, and something passed between them. The mood had turned serious—neither seemed able to look away.

Annie looked away first. "I should go."

Finn nodded as if he agreed that of course she should go, when in truth, he was wondering whether her cheek would feel as soft as it looked if he brushed it gently with his fingers.

Annie's eyes flitted to his then toward the door. "Well, okay." She got up and cleared the table.

Distracted, Finn managed to say, "I'll get that." But she'd already cleared everything and was well on her way to the kitchen.

Finn arrived at the kitchen island just as she turned to head for the door. Within inches of each other, they narrowly missed a collision. Finn grasped Annie's shoulders to steady her. Their eyes locked, and time seemed to stop. Lost for an instant, Finn recovered. "I'll walk you home."

"No," she answered a little too quickly. "Thanks, but I'll be fine."

It felt like they'd arrived on a doorstep at the end

of an awkward first date. Finn held the door open while she slipped past. Once outside, she turned and flashed an uneasy smile.

"Good night." Her voice sounded breathless.

"Good night, Annie." He watched until she was safely inside, then he went inside and shut the door.

What was that? For the most part, the evening had been fun like the old days. After all they'd been through, he felt sure their friendship had survived. But then there were glimpses of something else, something different between them.

He'd revealed too much of his feelings for her, and he'd made her feel awkward. If he wanted to preserve what was left of their friendship, he couldn't let that happen again.

6

The next afternoon, Annie walked into the retro chrome diner on the outskirts of town. Unchanged from her childhood memories, it felt like coming home. At a booth near the end of the counter, Regina Vestergaard, with her signature platinum pixie haircut and black-rimmed glasses, waved at Annie.

Annie grinned and walked to her, arms outstretched. As they hugged, Annie said, "It's so good to see you! I've missed you!"

"Me too."

Somewhere in the middle of catching up on their families, from Ella's elopement to Regi's boyfriend Derek to their latest work stories, they managed to order some lunch. When their food arrived, Regi held her fork suspended over her plate and asked nonchalantly, "So, you obviously saw him?"

Annie glanced at Regi. She prepared to dismiss the subject of Finn with a casual comment that, yes, she'd seen him, and then change the subject to anything else. But the direct, knowing look in her friend's eyes made it impossible—that and the way she said "*him*." Since middle school, they'd made a point of never saying his name. That way, the identity of her secret crush would never get out. Continuing the practice years later was more out of nostalgia than anything else.

Annie reluctantly smiled and stared down at her food. "Yes, I saw *him*. We had a sort of family meeting with our children about their decision to marry."

Regi's eyes opened wide. "Marry! And how did that go?"

"He's taking it better than I am." Annie exhaled. "There's nothing wrong with Connor, though. They seem happy enough."

"So far, a glowing endorsement. Go on."

"It's me. Watching Ella graduate and jump straight into marriage looks too familiar."

"But Ella's not you, and Connor is definitely not Matt."

"I know, but..."

"Which leaves you with two young people in love." Regi was sympathetic but frank.

Annie sighed. "Yeah, I guess."

"Do you really need to guess? If Connor is anything like his father, he'll be a great husband."

"It's a nice thought, but Connor has always struck me as being more like his mother's side of the family." She could see from the look on Regi's face that she didn't understand. How could she? Annie barely understood it herself. She couldn't blame Connor for being nothing like Finn. The world was full of wonderful people who weren't like Finn. And Georgina was not without her positive qualities. She was always stylishly dressed. She was always more pulled together than Annie. And Georgina could adroitly maneuver her way through the most difficult social situation. Annie envied her for that. But the qualities Annie valued most in people—things like kindness and selflessness, which Finn possessed— seemed to be lacking in Georgina. At least, Annie had never observed them in her.

She glanced up and discovered Regi staring with narrowing eyes. "Okay, so quick recap: Those two nutty kids announced they're getting married. Then you and Finn talked. Then what happened?"

Annie shrugged it off. "That's it. We talked about our children and marriage—their marriage." She completely left out their evening together and their

pact to spend the holiday season together. Why had
she done that?

Regi raised an eyebrow.

Annie inwardly cringed. This was coming out
wrong.

"And the divorce?"

Annie didn't expect that question. "You know
about that?"

Regi lifted her shoulders in a gesture that looked a
little smug. "I own a hair salon. It's like part town
crier and part priest's confessional."

"Wow! I didn't find out till he told me yesterday
morning!"

Regi's eyes lit with self-satisfaction, but it
changed to surprise. "Wait! You talked to him
yesterday morning? I thought you only were together
at that family meeting the night before last." Her
mouth turned up in one corner. "Or did that evening
talk last into the morning?"

"No!" That had come out too emphatically, so
she tried to soften the effect with a smirk and an eye
roll. "It's not what you're thinking." She proceeded to
tell the elopement story in detail but left out the
subsequent talk in the woods and their evening
together. She told herself there was nothing to tell,
but the truth was, she didn't want to share it.

Regi said simply, "He likes you."

"I like him too. Because we're friends. Friends like each other, and that's all we are. I have no desire to relive junior high—or high school, for that matter." She muttered under her breath, "Or college." *My twenties weren't all that great either.*

Regi gave her a half smile and raised her eyebrows. Annie couldn't blame her. After years of listening to Annie pine away over Finn, she had that and more coming. Beneath it all, Regi wanted her friend to be happy. Annie wanted to be happy too. Regrettably, that meant letting go of Finn, even if her heart still skipped a beat every time he looked at her. Now that they'd weathered the Ella-and-Connor elopement, Annie was determined to find contentment in being single.

Regi looked away with a glint in her eye. "Well, since you and Finn are just friends, you know that big Victorian house on the outskirts of town—the stunning one that's been on the market for months because no one here can afford it?"

"My dream home? Yeah, I know the one."

"Well, someone bought it. He's from Albany. I think he does something in state government."

"Palm-greasing and bribery?"

Regi nodded. "Well, whatever it is, he makes money. He came into the shop for a trim. Gorgeous thick black hair, graying temples, works out."

"His hair?"

"Ha. Very funny. He's got muscles, okay? Not too much, just the lean, sinewy kind."

"Got it. Muscles."

Regi shrugged and said in a singsong voice, "He is perfect for you. You should meet him. Just be thankful I'm in a relationship, or I'd be all over him like clippings on a barbershop floor."

Annie winced. "Sounds itchy."

Regi raised an eyebrow. "He'd be the guy to scratch it."

Annie held up her palms. "Let me stop you right there."

"But I was just getting to the good part!"

"I know. But this is the part where I shatter your dreams. Ella's off living her life, so I'm resetting mine —on my own. I'm content with my life. Why would I let some guy ruin it now?"

"Because he's got deep-set eyes you could drown in."

"But then I'd be dead."

"You'd die happy." Regi lifted an eyebrow. She launched into a familiar refrain. "You've been alone for the past twenty-one years. How much me time does one woman need?"

Annie smiled. "This amount."

With a sigh, Regi said, "Poor Alex Laghari. He'll be so disappointed."

Annie felt a pang of dread. "Regi, what have you done?"

Regi hastened to answer. "Nothing—except jot down his number from his appointment info, just in case." She leaned forward. "He's achingly attractive."

Annie sighed patiently. "He sounds like a real heartbreaker, but I already married one of those. I'm looking for something different—no drama. I don't want to date and feel scrutinized against some stranger's unknown expectations or have to sit through an evening with someone I wouldn't have spent five minutes chatting up at a cocktail party."

"Oh, come on. When's the last time you even went to a cocktail party?"

Annie leveled a look at her friend. "My point is: he sounds perfect. He's just not—"

"Finn?"

"I was going to say, 'Not perfect for me.'" Annie inwardly groaned. *No, not pity. Please don't look like that.*

Regi's voice rose in pitch. "Okay, I'll leave it alone. As long as you're happy. The thing is, I'm just having trouble believing you're happy."

Annie knew she meant well. Maybe she'd do the same for Regi if the tables were turned. But at the moment, Regi's friendly advice felt like unwelcome medicine. "I'm fine."

Regi peered over her glasses. "I can see that."

Annie smiled. "Thank you."

"For what?"

"Caring." The server put the check on the edge of the table. Annie grabbed it. "My treat."

"Okay, but it's my turn next time."

As they left the diner, they paused on the sidewalk. Regi said, "He really is attractive—by which I mean gorgeous."

Annie feigned ignorance. "Who?" She let go of the smirk she'd been holding back.

"Fine! It was worth a try, wasn't it?" Laughing, Regi shooed her away and headed toward her car.

Annie drove home with Regi's words echoing in her mind. Maybe she was right. It was time to move on. She was starting a new chapter in her life. She was content with her life as it was, but maybe she needed to be more open to change. It wasn't as though her mind was entirely closed to the possibility of meeting someone. But if something like that were meant to happen, it just seemed to Annie that it would happen organically, not by being set up by a friend or by using some sort of app like her daughter's friends used.

Annie walked inside and went straight to the refrigerator. "Mr. Willoughby, are you hungry?" She dished out some food and set it down for her cat. By this time, she would have heard the light padding of cat feet and felt Willoughby's fur on her ankles. "Mr. Willoughby?" She searched for him in all the usual places—his afternoon spot on the sun-drenched windowsill, the cozy tent in the corner—then all through the house. "Mr. Willoughby!" Panic set in. He must have slipped out when she left for lunch. That meant he'd been outside for hours in a woodsy area full of predators. She went outside and, calling his name, made her way around the cottage, searched behind shrubs and in the trees near the house. Her stomach sank as she went to the road and looked up and down the narrow country lane.

A screen door swung shut behind her. "Annie!"

She turned to find Finn holding her cat, with his paws resting comfortably over Finn's arms. Before she could ask, he said, "Look who stopped by for a visit while you were out."

Annie was riddled with guilt. "I didn't know he'd gotten out." She took the cat from Finn. "Mr. Willoughby, don't scare me like that."

Finn shrugged. "He's fine. Will and I—"

"Will?"

His mouth quirked at the corner. "Yeah, we're bros now. Anyway, we both had some tuna for lunch and a nice walk down to the creek, then we hung out and watched ESPN. He loved it! But I had to draw the line at painting his face in team colors. He took it hard, but he got over it."

Annie didn't quite disapprove, but she wasn't on board with it either. "Mr. Willoughby's more of a costume-drama sort of guy."

Finn shook his head. "He said you'd say that." He leaned closer. "He's not."

Annie looked down at her cat. "Maybe we could compromise and find you a nice quiet golf game to watch." She glanced in Finn's direction and begrudgingly added, "Or a fishing show."

"He likes fish."

Annie laughed. "I had a feeling he might." She lifted her eyes to meet Finn's. "Thanks for rescuing him."

"No problem."

They parted ways, but when Annie reached her front door, she stole a glance back at Finn. She didn't expect him to look over at her, but he did, and an awkward wave followed.

7

Finn arrived home from a run. With hands stiff from the cold, he fumbled with the door key while his breath filled the air with a mist. Once inside, he got a fire going in the wood stove and sat down in his favorite chair that looked out at the trees lining the creek. This was what he'd come here for. So why couldn't he feel the peace that he saw all around him? It was going to take time. He knew that, but knowing it wasn't enough.

His phone rang, and he winced when he saw who the caller was. He sighed then answered. "Georgina."

"Hi, Finn."

This was his cue to speak, but he just didn't feel like it. They'd parted ways on relatively good terms— as good as terms could be when your wife leaves you for some other guy. But he'd been miserable for so long during the marriage, he surprised himself by how little he felt. After he got over the shock, he numbly moved on with his life.

His lawyer told him he was caving too easily on the property settlement. But the last thing he wanted was to drag out that thing. So he gave her the house and nearly everything in it including the car in the garage, and what little was left they split down the middle. No doubt this was why she'd been so amiable through the whole thing. She had no right to complain.

"Finn? Are you there?"

"Yeah."

With a nervous laugh, she said, "Oh, I thought the call dropped."

"No, I'm here."

"Well, I wanted to tell you before you heard it somewhere else."

Finn slowly blinked and stared at the fire.

"So... I'm getting married."

"To whom?"

"To Adam!"

He smirked. He knew who. She'd left him for Adam. He was just busting her chops. *First Connor, now you. Is anyone else getting married?* He bit his tongue and instead said, "Congratulations."

"Thanks."

She sounded uncomfortable. *Good.*

"So, I just thought you should hear it from me."

"Okay. Thanks for calling. Look, I can't talk now. I'm on my way out the door." *Sometime in the next twenty-four hours.*

"I'll let you go then. Bye, Finn."

"Bye."

He hung up the phone and set it down on the table beside him. "I wish you all the happiness you deserve." He smirked and stared out the window.

The night Georgina broke the news that she was leaving him for Adam, Finn had just gotten home from working a protest in Manhattan, so his day had already been lousy. He struggled to stay awake on the hour-long commute to their home in Putnam County. Once home, he went straight to the shower. Peaceful protests weren't at all what they used to be. Now protestors threw bags of urine at cops. He supposed that was easier for them than framing a logical argument. By the end of the evening, a hot shower felt good. He'd barely finished throwing on some clothes when Georgina told him she was leaving him. That was a memorable day.

After that, and a few more peaceful protests that wounded a dozen fellow officers, he was done. He was lucky. The broken bricks and debris hurled at him only left him with bruises and burnout. But his marriage was over, his job wasn't what he signed up for, and his son didn't need him anymore. He had enough years in, so he'd retired.

Now here he was. Alone in the family vacation A-frame. Alone wasn't bad. Everything that had made him unhappy was hours away and unable to touch him. After the pain subsided, the numbness felt good. And that seemed to be where he remained—in a state of numbness.

His phone dinged with an incoming text. He glanced toward it and almost decided to ignore it. *What if it's Connor?* He picked it up and grinned. It was a picture of Annie and him in the summer after second grade, both sporting red stains on their faces from eating cherry popsicles. He couldn't stop smiling.

He texted, *Life doesn't get any better than that!*

Sadness gripped him as he realized it was true.

Annie sat on the floor of her attic, surrounded by forgotten treasures whose value lay deep in her heart. She set aside the old snapshot she'd texted to Finn and put the lid on the box. Organizing those photos would be a perfect rainy-day project. She moved on to a box with her name on it. Inside, she found all the trinkets and dried flowers that had seemed so important when she was in high school. The whole point of this attic endeavor was to clear out unwanted items and organize what was left. With an empty trash bag and full boxes, she wasn't doing very well. She had to get ruthless. She managed to throw away some dried flowers that fell apart in her hands. She reached in for more and found her old journal.

Keeping a diary had seemed like the thing for a teenage girl to do. That was six months before she'd decided the last thing she wanted to do was leave a record of her pathetic one-way crush. She ran her fingers along the jagged remains of the ripped-out journal pages and let out a bitter laugh. Shredding hadn't been enough. She recalled how she went into the bathroom and set the papers on fire and part of a hand towel with them. Her method of disposal may have been flawed, but she'd made the right choice. She would always remember what that journal had contained. There were no lovely sonnets or inspired passages of prose. It was just raw emotion, the echoes of which she could still feel now.

Annie thought she heard something downstairs. Then she heard Finn's voice yelling her name. She yelled down to him. "I'm up here in the attic. Come on up."

Finn rounded the top of the stairs. "I got some of

your mail. It's on the table downstairs. The regular mail carrier must be on vacation."

Spying the pile of photos before her, he joined her on the floor and picked up one to examine. "Who took all these?"

"Weren't we adorable? My mother was forever trying to chronicle every moment of our childhood existence. In the process, I think she missed out on the real-time experience. But she got some great pics, didn't she?"

They spent the next half hour gasping and laughing as they looked through a few dozen photos.

When a lull settled between them, Finn asked, "So, what are you doing up here?"

"My goal was to thin out my inventory, but everything has a memory. I have a hard time letting go. You know?"

He seemed puzzled. "Not really."

It was her turn to look puzzled. Before she could ask, he said, "I guess that's why I moved up from Mahopac full time."

Annie hesitated. "I wondered about that. It's a pretty long commute."

"A little over an hour." His expression clouded over as he hesitated. "I moved here to get away from everything—except Connor." He glanced at her then went on. "So I guess I'm the opposite of you."

She knew him too well to believe that. "But you came here for a reason. Maybe memories?"

He nearly smiled, but it faded as quickly as it had appeared. "Or a free place to live."

"Free is good, but I know you. There's more to it than that."

A long silence followed. Annie waited. Something was going on with him. She'd noticed it the day after their children's engagement announcement. He seemed weighed down by it. Maybe that's why he was taking the engagement so well.

Finn said, "You're right, as usual."

Annie wanted to tease him and make him repeat the sentiment, but he looked so grim that she let it go.

"I retired."

"Retired? You're only forty-three."

"I only needed twenty years to retire. I worked twenty-two."

"Wow, I'm in the wrong field." She instantly regretted her words. "I didn't mean that. I'm just being... stupid."

"For a cop, the years are like dog years. Every year on the job feels like seven." Finn stared straight ahead with lifeless eyes. "If you'd asked me a couple years ago if I planned to retire at this age, I would've said no."

Annie wanted to say something encouraging or comforting, but she couldn't find the words.

Finn combed his fingers through his hair. "On the plus side, they didn't even have to defund the police. The retirements and resignations did the job for them. And now look at the city."

Annie's heart ached to see Finn like this. He'd always been the kind of guy people turned to because he was willing to lend a hand, and he brought a positive approach to any situation. The man before her had been beaten down emotionally—and probably physically too. She'd seen enough videos of riots and cities on fire to imagine what he must have been through.

She noticed a small scar on his forehead that hadn't been there before. Tentatively, she pointed at it. "Was that from work?"

"Flying brick versus forehead. The brick won." He tried to smile, but it didn't reach his eyes.

Without thinking, she reached out and touched the scar. He moved too slightly to call it a flinch. His eyes met hers, and something palpable happened between them. It was so unexpected, Annie's breath caught in her throat. He appeared as stunned as she felt. His lips parted.

Finn's phone rang. His eyes flickered away as though he didn't know what to do next. He recovered and pulled out his phone. He still looked like he was in shock when he said, "I've got to go."

Annie helplessly watched as he answered the phone and went back down the stairs.

What was that?

She leaned back against a stack of boxes and caught her breath.

You are not going to torture yourself. She wasn't a schoolgirl anymore. She was an adult. And one of the great benefits of being an adult was that she knew better than to do this to herself. She forced herself to think clearly. Finn had been through a traumatic series of events. He was vulnerable, and he trusted her. They trusted each other, which was why, no matter what that might have been, it wasn't too late. They hadn't done anything foolish. Like kiss.

What if I've misread the whole situation?

By the time Finn reached the bottom step, a recording came on his phone trying to sell him a car warranty. He shoved his phone back in his pocket, glanced back up the empty staircase, and nearly tripped over the cat as he walked out the door.

He had crossed over into an alternate universe.

What else could explain what just happened? It was
a moment.

A moment? I nearly leaned over and kissed her!

Once inside his cabin, he put on his headphones
and tried to drown out his thoughts with his playlist
of nineties alternative rock. Three songs later, he lay
sprawled on his sofa staring at the ceiling. It wasn't
working. He pulled off his headphones and gave in to
his thoughts.

How had that even happened? He'd been talking
about his retirement, and she felt sorry for him. He
hadn't meant to elicit her pity, but Annie was inher-
ently empathetic. He couldn't blame her for that.
The more he thought about it, sympathy and attrac-
tion could look a lot alike. Both involved gazing with
soft, caring expressions, and her eyes had looked soft
and caring. That must have been it. It was sympathy.
He'd only misconstrued it because of his feelings for
her. That made sense.

Those feelings presented an issue. Finn wasn't
one to lie to himself. He'd loved her for years. He
once assumed it would all fade away, but years
passed. It wasn't as though she was on his mind
constantly. He'd been wrapped up in his life. Children had a way of making it easy to put one's
thoughts and needs on a figurative shelf. But from
time to time, something would bring back a memory.

There was something comforting about that. The past was a secret place he could escape to and remember what happiness felt like. He lived for the summers when he would see her or even exchange a few words. He tried to rationalize his emotions by telling himself she was just Annie, part of what made being up here in the mountains so special—like the sweet smell of grass and earth just as a summer rain starts to fall. This was where he felt peace, and Annie was part of it all.

Being back at the cabin full-time had changed everything. Finn was single again, for one thing, and his son had gone on with his life. He wasn't working, so he had time to think—too much time. And Annie wasn't just in his past any longer. She was right there next door, practically within reach. His once-pleasant memory of the past was now present.

And yet it seemed fitting that she would be there. Their friendship was solid and comfortable, the sort that could survive separation for years and resume where they'd left off when they got back together. A friendship like that was a valuable thing. Trying to shoehorn it into something else was too much of a risk. One weak moment of longing to put his lips on hers wasn't worth acting on and losing a friendship over.

Still, they'd had that moment. It was too powerful

to try to pretend it hadn't happened. It was going to make things awkward between them. The more time that passed before seeing each other, the more awkward it would become. He wasn't sure what he could do about that. Except see her. Like ripping off a Band-Aid, they needed to see each other soon and do something that would feel normal again. At this moment, he couldn't imagine anything that would make him feel normal. He'd have to figure that out. He and Annie might not ever forget how they'd felt at that moment. He certainly wouldn't. But if they could view it as a passing aberration, their friendship would survive, as solid and reliable as always. With any luck, his feelings for her would go quietly back to the place in his heart where they belonged—safely buried.

8

Annie stole glances at Finn's cabin while raking the last remnants of leaves from her yard. She had left it too long, but the first snow had melted and given her a second chance to clear the leaves.

Two days had passed since she'd seen him. That wasn't unusual for neighbors, but Finn was her friend. She missed him. That wasn't unusual either. Annie surveyed her progress and decided she'd done enough raking for the season. After putting the rake away, she emerged from the garage. There he was at the mailbox.

Finn seemed happy to see her. The resulting warmth in her chest was an overreaction, but she couldn't help it. Since their little attic event, Annie's insecurity had taken hold. She prided herself on being an expert at controlling her feelings. Why she had let her guard down like that, even if only for a moment, she still couldn't understand. It was obviously awkward for Finn. She even wondered if he had some sort of app on his phone that had caused it to ring with one touch. She couldn't bear the thought of him having to escape from her like that. It was a step beyond looking at your watch and saying, "Oh, look at the time." She wondered if Finn was avoiding her now. *No, that's impossible.* But she had a superstitious fear that if she said it or thought it enough, it might come true.

Seeing him now reassured her.

He waved, mail in hand. "Annie!"

She waved back. Happiness washed over her. She'd missed his easy smile.

He walked over to her and stood close enough for her to catch a whiff of his soap. She stifled an urge to lean forward, fling her arms about his waist, and bury her face in his chest.

Finn's eyes seemed intent on her. Was he having a similar thought? No, he pulled a dead leaf out of her hair, then he lifted his mail. "Look at this."

With a puzzled grin, she stated the obvious. "That looks like an envelope."

He glared into her eyes, but a mischievous spark betrayed his amusement. A moment passed. When she failed to produce the correct response, he said, "It's a Christmas card."

"That's nice." She could immediately see that was the wrong thing to say.

He looked earnestly at her and repeated, "It's a Christmas card."

Confused, she said, "Yes. I think we've established that."

"Which means...?"

"It's a card... about Christmas?" She was really trying to grasp the point he was making.

"Which means Christmas is coming."

Annie raised her eyebrows, which prompted a disapproving sigh from Finn. "Oh, I get it," he said. "You're one of those people who has their Christmas shopping done in July."

You don't know me at all. Even if that were true, I would never admit it. "I'm actually not much of a shopper. It's my only character flaw."

"That's great!"

"I know! As flaws go, it's way better than sloth."

His eyebrows drew together. "Yeah. Too bad, though."

Annie brushed her hair back. "Really? It's never been a problem before."

"Because we've never been together at Christmas."

Together? That sounds like a promotion from neighbor. "No, I guess not."

His face lit up as if a light bulb had just gone on in his brain. "Misery loves company!"

"Good to know. A stitch in time saves nine." Annie glanced back at her cottage. This was not one of their more sensible conversations. Still, any conversation with Finn was a good one.

He was smiling that broad, spontaneous smile that always lit his face and invariably hers. "So we should go Christmas shopping together!"

"Sure. We should do that."

"How does tomorrow morning sound? We could grab some breakfast then press our noses to the glass until the stores open."

That sounded just perfect, except for one thing. She winced. "Tomorrow's a workday. I'm not on vacation till the end of the week."

"Oh. I forgot that you work since you're here all the time."

Annie nodded. "Working from home. But I could go after work."

Finn shook his head. "Won't you be tired?"

"That's okay. I still need to do my Christmas shopping—not that I'll get it all done in one evening, but it's a start."

Finn folded his arms and stared off in the

distance. "Yeah, and what we don't get done tomorrow, we can finish this weekend."

"I guess we could do that." It sounded like a perfectly good idea. She just hadn't expected the offer.

"Good! It's a date—a *shopping* date. Call me when you clock out of work."

"Okay."

As she went inside, the word *date* echoed in her mind. *A shopping date's almost a date. It has the word "date" in it, so that's good enough.*

No, it wasn't. It wasn't good at all. For someone who was determined to focus on herself for the first time in years, the bulk of her thoughts went to Finn. Maybe thinking about Finn was just an unhealthy habit she'd carried over from youth, like leaves that don't get raked away in the fall.

Oh my gosh! My brain's full of leaves! You can rake all you want, but you're never fully rid of them. You might think that they're gone, then it snows, and for months, you forget them. Then spring comes, and there they are—all wet and mushy, and smothering healthy grass so it can't grow up and live a full life. I've got Finn-induced leaf rot, and it's keeping me from living a full life in the sun.

It had to be some kind of syndrome. She fully

expected to find it on the next cover of *Psychology Today*.

But eventually, leaves decompose and fertilize the soil, which is good. Except that means my brain is full of... fertilizer.

Finding herself once again caught up in a familiar emotional cycle, Annie applied the only known cure. She went to the kitchen and cooked up a pot of hot chocolate, filled her favorite Christmas mug, and topped it off with whipped cream. On the way to the sofa, she grabbed a pair of fuzzy socks and a throw blanket then settled down by the fire to watch a holiday movie.

9

It was no use. Flutters of anticipation plagued Annie throughout the workday, and it wasn't from work. She didn't mind her job as an insurance biller, but it wasn't exactly the kind of work that made one feel tingly all over.

Finn, on the other hand, did. Each time her heart tried to take flight, Annie reminded herself they were only going shopping. Even if they'd be spending the evening together, Christmas shopping placed them firmly in the friend zone. Given the past couple of days, a return to familiar territory would be a relief. Annie rolled her eyes. She'd had a lifetime of that familiar territory, but overanalyzing a ten-second event in the attic was torture.

The truth was, if she and Finn were meant to be together, it wouldn't be so hard. People met all the time, and they knew which path they were on. Even if things didn't work out, they knew where they stood. But she and Finn were just aimlessly wandering. They really needed a path.

For two days, she had wasted valuable time she would never get back simply trying to second-guess Finn, which was something she'd never done well. Nothing tangible or measurable had happened between them, except one or both of them had tried to fly too close to the sun. Relationships were complicated and potentially painful. Friendships were consistent and reliable. So here they were, where they belonged. It was good to be on familiar footing.

Annie was ready and sipping a coffee when Finn arrived at the door, looking like an outdoorsy magazine ad. He wore outdoor gear as a rule, but today, his jeans were freshly laundered, and his pullover knit shirt fit just snugly enough to define the muscles in his shoulders. She wouldn't mind giving him a few more of those shirts for Christmas. His hair stuck out in damp clumps, not yet dry from the shower, and a subtle whiff of cologne wafted toward her. She breathed in through her nostrils.

His eyes swept over her face. "Ready?"

"Yes." As they walked to the car, she marveled at how shopping with a friend could feel so suspiciously like a date.

Two hours of wandering from store to store cured Annie of any preconceived notion that this was a date. It was way too much fun for that. As small as Cedar Creek was, it went all out for Christmas, with evergreens and lights lining both sides of Main Street. Every store had its own charming Christmas display. Annie couldn't imagine how anyone could walk down the sidewalks without being infused with Christmas spirit.

Finn and Annie got so caught up in the holiday spirit that they began to compete for who could find the weirdest gift and then to identify who deserved to receive it. They realized it was time to go home when Annie was laughing so hard she had to apologize to the store clerk ringing them up, after which Finn grasped Annie's hand and led her outside.

As Finn settled into the driver's seat, Annie said, "I still think the cowboy-boot toilet brush holder had your name written all over it."

"You, madam, have succumbed to a bad case of shopping hysteria."

Annie frowned. "Which isn't a thing."

"But hunger is. How 'bout something to eat?"

"Sure."

In the middle of town, they settled into a booth in a cozy cafe, where they reviewed their shopping lists and formed a plan of attack for the following weekend. Annie took her last sip of hot chocolate. "Christmas shopping was never this fun, although if Ella asks, tell her I said she's my favorite shopping companion. I could never drag Matt into stores." *Why did I even bring up his name?*

"Matt never struck me as the gift-shopping type." He hastened to add, "Most guys aren't. I'm not. I guess that's why I clown around so much. It's a coping mechanism."

"I think shopping was too mundane for Matt." She lifted her eyes to meet Finn's. Being friends for so long wasn't always a good thing. He seemed to know there was more, so he waited. "Matt never did anything in an ordinary way—including dying. He was good at surprises." Annie drew in a breath. "I don't know where that came from. I'm sorry."

"Why?"

Compassion was a powerful thing. In the right hands, it could pierce any armor. It certainly cut through Annie's. "Because."

"Good answer." His mouth turned up at the corners.

She'd meant to say more—something to smooth over the moment and veer the conversation in a different direction—but she couldn't speak for a second. No matter what she'd been through with Matt, random moments still gripped her.

"Matt and I weren't happy." That was no deep, dark secret that she was disclosing. Matt had done everything in a grand way, including argue. He didn't have a violent bone in his body, but he was dramatic. In retrospect, Annie realized all the excitement and energy she'd been drawn to at the start had a flip side. When things didn't go his way, Matt's energy had been equally strong. "At the time, I let my emotions drive my decisions. That was a mistake and a tough lesson to learn."

Finn nodded with compassion, which almost overwhelmed her.

"When Matt died, I just took that part of my life and gently packed it away. It would be there if I ever needed to remember, but I didn't want to." She stopped. "I'm sorry. I don't know why I'm telling you this."

Finn said simply, "Because I'm your friend."

How could the same words make her feel so cared for yet kept at arm's length? "It's this place—being home. I can't seem to shake the sensation that I've stepped back in time, and the oddest memories come back with no warning. I still walk into the kitchen and see my grandfather holding a green Fiestaware mug full of coffee. For some reason, that makes me choke up. This village is full of things like that—little breadcrumbs people left behind, marking their journeys. And me. I'm left behind."

Finn's eyes softened. "I'm here too."

"I think I've always known you were there for me —even when I didn't like what you had to say."

His eyebrows creased as though he didn't understand when that might have happened.

Annie felt the need to explain. "When you told me I shouldn't have married Matt, I was angry. I think I might have overreacted."

"Do you mean when you said I was jealous?"

Annie grimaced.

He went on. "And that I didn't want anyone else to be happy?"

Annie winced. "I was wrong. You were right."

Finn smiled gently. "Let's engrave that on something. It would make a great Christmas gift."

She would've laughed if she weren't so embarrassed.

Finn's smile faded. He clenched his jaw, which he usually did when he was stressed. Or lying. Annie narrowed her eyes. "What?"

"I didn't say anything."

"But you're thinking it. Come on, Finn. I know you. You're a terrible liar."

He combed his fingers through his hair. "I'm not

lying. I don't even know what you think I'm lying about."

"I think you're not telling me something." She assumed he was sparing her feelings. She could only imagine what else he might've said.

He exhaled. "Dammit, Annie. Okay, I was jealous!"

His words dealt such a harsh blow, she froze. *Is this one of Finn's jokes?*

He shrugged. "I never told you the whole story about Europe."

Still in shock, Annie waited and listened.

Finn continued. "Tamara dumped me in Amsterdam. I hung around there for a week. During that week, I kept thinking of you. Then I cut short the trip and booked a flight back to New York."

"Thinking of *me*?"

His eyes darted about like they always did when he was nervous. "Don't laugh, but I got it in my head that I... missed you."

Don't laugh? I can't even breathe.

"I know. It's crazy. Chalk it up to temporary insanity. I think I was homesick, and you're part of what I think of as home."

That would've been a nice thing to hear if her ears hadn't been ringing. She'd tried to shake her head when he said it was crazy that he'd kept thinking of her. Then she just gave up trying to respond. A wave of nausea washed over her.

He gazed off to the distance and smiled his winning smile, but it was forced. "Lucky you! I was going to tell you, but by the time I got home, you'd run off to get married. You dodged a bullet there, Oakley."

This was the part where she needed to say something, but she felt breathless and sick. "Excuse me a minute." Surprised by how normal she sounded, she managed to slip out of the restaurant booth before she lost her composure. Once in the bathroom, she closed the stall door and exhaled. Why was he telling her this now? She would've been better off not knowing. And yet the idea that he had cared even briefly meant something. If she hadn't been in such a vulnerable state over Finn, she would never have fallen so hard for Matt and agreed to get married. Finn might've come home and told her how he felt, and they could've been something to each other. She couldn't think of that now. She needed to pull it together and get home without falling apart.

By the time she got back to the table, Finn had paid for the check. Annie didn't bother to protest. She did manage a quick, "I'll buy next time." Then she realized there would be a next time, and soon. They had plans for a whole day of shopping together on Saturday. That didn't give her much time to recover, but she would—because she would have to.

Or she could make up an excuse.

The ride home was awkwardly quiet. Finn gripped the steering wheel and stared straight ahead. After an unbearable silence, he said, "Things worked out okay, didn't they?"

Annie turned and stared at him as if he'd lost his mind. "My husband died, you got divorced, and our children have run off and gotten married without thinking it through. I don't know. I guess you could say things worked out."

"Oh, crap. I'm an idiot. I didn't mean anything about Matt."

"I know. I made it sound worse." Annie took pity on him. "I'm not sure why I did that." She had the feeling they'd both walked out on a tightrope and weren't sure whether to go the rest of the way or turn back.

His mention of Matt brought a memory to the surface. "It meant a lot to me when you came to the funeral. I was drifting about in a daze, and then you were there. You were my anchor. I don't even know what I said or did that day, but I knew you were there." She turned and stared out the window as the car lights grew blurry.

Finn gave her hand a squeeze. "It was nothing you wouldn't do for me."

For the remainder of the ride home, Annie's mood vacillated. One minute, fear coursed through her chest as she felt their friendship changing in ways that might damage it. The next minute, she wanted to tell him to pull over so she could climb on him before he could defend himself. She'd never been a climb-onto-a-guy sort of girl, so the logistics involved kept her from acting upon it. She wasn't as limber as she'd been in her twenties. But she thought about it. A lot.

But what she and Finn had now was valuable and rare, built on a long history that proved it to be solid and reliable. That made it sound boring. It was anything but. There were heart-throbbing moments that could make a girl believe in fairy tales. Except the men in fairy tales were always strangers, which was why those stories could never come true. Once the fairy-tale couples got to know one another, they'd probably break up and move on. But with Finn, it was real. There was little they didn't know about one another.

And he lived right next door. In theory, it was an ideal situation, but what if it backfired? If something happened between them, they'd still be stuck seeing each other. Going to the mailbox or taking out the trash would become intolerable. Annie sighed. Were they meant to be friends, or could they mean something more to each other? Her track record hadn't infused her with confidence. All she wanted was to make the right choice. Couldn't someone just tell her? Was that too much to ask?

Finn pulled into the driveway and parked. "I'll walk you home."

Her knee-jerk reaction was to protest, but she caught herself. He was being gallant, and she liked it. He would do the same for his ninety-year-old grandmother if he had one. *Calm down. He's just being Finn.*

They proceeded to have the most mundane conversation they'd ever had. The weather got them halfway there. Then they talked about when and where they'd go Christmas shopping and who they'd shop for. If this had been a first date, Annie would have had doubts. *But it's not a first date. Why are you even comparing it to a date?* Maybe it was the electric charge that practically arced between them? They had walked this walk dozens—maybe hundreds—of times. And yet, this was different.

They stopped outside the door. Annie unlocked it and turned back. She was going to ask him in for a beer or a coffee, but when she looked into his eyes, her brain went numb. She was all nerve endings and wild emotions.

He gazed at her until she thought she'd melt into the door. "It feels..."

Exhilarating? Romantic?

"Weird." A bashful smile started to form on his lips. "Doesn't it?"

Annie took in the view for a moment—really nice lips, full and in perfect proportion to the rest of his face.

He continued, "I mean, we've been next door every summer all these years, but we've been caught up in our separate lives. It's been a long time since we've spent time together like this—like we used to."

"We grew up. Everything changed."

His eyes bored through her. So much for the I'm-a-strong-woman-with-everything-under-control vibe she'd been trying to project. If he so much as touched her, she might melt or fall in a dead faint.

He said, "But the connection is still there."

For one dizzying moment, she almost managed a nod.

Finn leaned his shoulder against the door frame. "If you think of how much we've changed, it only makes sense that our friendship would change along with it."

"It has." Annie was relieved to hear that her voice didn't reveal all the turmoil inside.

Finn's eyes locked on her. "I just wonder... do you ever wonder..."

Annie lifted her eyebrows as if that would help him finish his thought.

"What if?"

If she didn't feel so awkward, she would've burst out laughing. *"What if?" Have I ever wondered "what if?"* As if that weren't her favorite pastime from, oh, maybe the age of twelve until... now. "What if... what?" *Breathe.*

"What if us? What if we..." His eyes trailed down to her lips.

She didn't mean to part her lips in response. But her lips had gone rogue along with the rest of her body. *What if we... kissed?*

He leaned closer. She leaned into him.

Blinding headlights covered them in a blaze of white light. Either they'd crossed over and that was the bright light they should follow, or it was a car pulling into the driveway for a late-evening visit.

Finn exhaled with enough exasperation to fill Annie with hope that he'd wanted the kiss as much as she had. Doors opened on both sides of the car.

"Mom?"

"Ella." No one had ever told Annie that the awful

timing children had would continue long into adulthood.

Ella pulled her overnight bag from the back seat, slammed the car door, and marched toward the cottage. Connor hung back, arms crossed over his chest.

Finn said, "Connor? What's going on?"

Connor leveled an icy look at his father.

Ella asked, "Mom, can I just go inside, please?"

Only then did Annie realize that she was blocking the door. "Oh, sorry." She glanced at Finn with a helpless shrug.

He met her look with his own unvoiced frustration. "Good night, Annie."

Annie watched him turn and follow Connor back to his cabin.

Why? Why me?

10

Ella sat at the kitchen table while Annie made coffee. "There's nothing to talk about. Our marriage is just not working out."

"What happened to 'you've been together for four years and have known each other all your lives'?"

"Yeah, I thought I knew him, but marriage is different, I guess."

Annie scooped the coffee grounds into the filter, turned on the coffee maker, then leaned on the counter, facing Ella. "How so?"

Ella narrowed her eyes. "I don't know. He's changed."

"In a week?" Annie forced the shocked look off her face. This was clearly a crisis for Ella, and she didn't want to make her feel judged. She remembered how difficult her own marriage had been, but Connor was different. He couldn't be anything like Matt. "Have you tried waiting until you've both calmed down and then trying to talk?"

"Having a talk about how you just blew up something doesn't mean you can put it back together."

"That sounds a little extreme."

"How hard is it to get an annulment?"

Annie hoped she wasn't serious, but Ella sure wasn't smiling. "I don't know what's in the wedding vows that you said in Las Vegas, but usually, there's something in there like *till death do you part.*"

Ella muttered, "Don't give me any ideas." But she lifted her eyes to her mother's wide eyes, and a hint of a smile teased her mouth.

Annie poured two cups of coffee and handed one to Ella. "Have you thought about counseling?"

Ella stared at her mother as if she were nuts. "That's why I'm here!"

Annie inwardly squirmed. "I'm not really trained for this sort of thing, and it sounds like you need a professional."

"Did you ever see one?"

"No. And see how that worked out?" She smiled gently, and it worked. Ella smiled back, but only briefly.

"Ella, I love you, and I want to help. I will if I can. But there are people who actually know what they're talking about when it comes to this stuff."

Ella shook her head, so Annie didn't pursue it. "Does Connor feel the same way?"

"I'm pretty sure he hates me."

"It seems to me it should take longer than this to work up a good case of hatred against the person you've just married."

Ella's eyebrows looked stuck in a creased position. "Connor is a very quick study."

Annie took a sip of coffee and glanced out the window at Finn's cabin. Were he and Connor having the same conversation? "So, whose idea was it to come here?"

"Mine. I was going to drive here by myself, but Connor said I was too upset to drive, so he drove me, which obviously means he wasn't upset. Which means he hates me."

Annie squinted. "I don't think so." She had a strong urge to laugh, but that would have been the worst thing to do. Somehow, she managed to keep a straight face. "You might be missing a few links in that chain of logic."

"Well, maybe I'm not explaining it well, but the end result is the same."

Annie gave her a questioning look.

"He hates me," Ella said.

Annie nodded. "He must hate you a lot to drive up here from Mahopac just to make sure you got here safely."

Ella wasn't buying it. "No, he's got that unfailing sense of duty and honor, just like his father."

Annie smiled. She had a point there. Finn was the kind of guy who helped people and did the right thing, no matter how it inconvenienced him. She had watched Connor grow up. She might not have been in favor of his hasty marriage to Ella, but Connor wouldn't have done it if he didn't love her. Annie had a feeling that they'd just gotten ahead of themselves. "My mother used to say, 'Don't let the sun go down on your anger.' I thought she was brilliant until I discovered it's in the Bible. It's not bad advice."

Ella gave Annie a dose of her old teenage disdain. "Don't look now, but it's dark out, so too late for that."

Annie said wryly, "They went to bed early back then."

Ella looked at her mother and wrinkled her face.

Annie said, "Go talk to him."

Ella heaved a sigh. "I don't know. I'm too tired to argue. Couldn't I just rest up and start again in the morning?"

A knock sounded on the kitchen door. Connor's

muffled voice called out, "Ella?" If Stanley Kowalski had been sheepish, he would have sounded exactly like Connor.

Annie peered at Ella with a questioning look and received a reluctant nod in return. After Annie let Connor in, she felt a sudden desire to be anywhere else. The cottage was small, and those two needed privacy to hash out their issues. Finn was involved in all this as much as she was, so comparing notes might fill in some of the gaps in the story. Convinced it might help resolve matters, she grabbed her jacket from a hook by the door and headed over to Finn's.

But as she arrived on Finn's stoop, she relived the moments before Ella and Connor pulled into the driveway.

Do you ever wonder what if?

She hadn't knocked yet. There was still time to slink home and hide out in her bedroom. But what if Finn saw her on the way over? Ordinarily, she'd assume that he hadn't, but with Connor at her place, he might look out the window and wonder how things were going. But he might not have looked out the exact moment Annie crossed the driveway to his yard. And there was no snow on the ground, so she wouldn't even leave any footprints. Still, if he did happen to see her walk over and back, it would make things even weirder than they already were. Logic aside, the idea to flee was tempting.

Finn opened the door and stepped aside, gesturing for her to come in, which she did. "So, what's going on over there? I figure by now, they're either killing each other or having newlywed sex all over your cottage."

"Ew!" She was too appalled to even consider the look on her face, but Finn laughed.

"Finn! It's not funny. It's gross." She walked to the window and looked toward her cottage. "I'd like to think it's not just a binary choice. There must be other options along that continuum."

With twinkling eyes, Finn said, "You're right. They're probably just making out in the food-prep area of your kitchen."

Any scowled. "Thanks. You know, I came here for support."

He laughed. "Oh, come on! Don't lie to me. You came here to escape!"

She didn't know how he could find this so funny. She was upset and dismayed—and a dozen other emotions. But he did have a point. "Maybe a little. Seriously, I thought they needed some privacy. Who wants to fight when their mother-in-law is standing there? Oh my gosh."

At least he stopped smiling. "What?"

"I'm a mother-in-law."

"So? I'm a father-in-law."

He wasn't getting this at all. "Nobody makes jokes about fathers-in-law."

He tilted his head, conceding her point. But then he crossed his arms and put his fist under his chin as though he were deep in thought. "Hmm. Why is that?"

Seeing where this was going, Annie said, "I'm not like that."

"Like what?"

"Like whatever it is mothers-in-law act like that makes people not like them." She was being serious, and it bothered her that he wasn't.

Finn put his hands on her shoulders. "I'm kidding. You're not like that. Come on, let's go sit down."

While Annie sat on the sofa, Finn added a log to the fire. When it was sufficiently blazing, he sat down beside her. "Do you know what I think?"

She lifted doubtful eyes to meet his but didn't answer.

"I think you worry too much. If those two made it through college, they can probably figure out marriage."

"We didn't." *That sounded weird.* "I mean, our two marriages didn't work out so well."

For someone who had taken everything pretty lightly until now, Finn was suddenly serious. "No, but those two are different."

"I hope so."

"They can't do much worse than Georgina and I did."

That wasn't exactly breaking news. Finn and his wife weren't the sort to make big scenes in public, but there were little things Annie had noticed. Finn would walk out the back door and head for the creek. A few minutes later, his wife would come out, search the trees that lined the creek, and apparently give up and go back inside. It might've been nothing, but Annie always got the impression they'd been arguing. Annie wasn't big on public displays of affection, either, but those two never touched. They'd looked like two coworkers raising a child.

Over the years, Annie had done her best to lock the Matt years away where she wouldn't have to think about them. But now it all seemed to come back. "I don't think Matt and I would've made it."

Finn didn't look surprised.

"I used to wonder what he thought, but then one day, I realized he didn't think about me at all."

"I never liked him. To be honest, I never understood why you married him."

Annie did, but she couldn't explain it to Finn.

Without meaning to, and without ever knowing, Finn had broken her heart. She took care to keep that out of her explanation. "Matt swept me off my feet. He was bigger than life, and at that point in mine, that looked pretty appealing. I should've taken the time to get to know him better. Then I would've figured it out —at least I hope I would have. But one day, he completely surprised me and said, 'Let's get married.' Before I recovered from that, he said, 'Let's run away and get married this weekend!'"

"Just like that?"

Annie looked straight at Finn. "Just like Connor and Ella."

Finn slowly blinked and shook his head. "Which is why their marriage touched a raw nerve."

With an understanding nod, Annie said, "Connor's great. I just hope he's great for Ella. Neither of them has had very good role models in the marriage department."

"That's a sobering thought. So you're basically saying they're doomed."

"No, they'll be fine." She said it emphatically, overcompensating for her nagging doubt.

"And how will you be?"

She hadn't seen that question coming. She wasn't sure how to react. "I'll be fine. I'm always fine." *That was a lie.*

He gazed at her intently. "You are, aren't you? You've managed to raise a child on your own, and you've made it look easy."

It was Annie's turn to chuckle. "Well, that was all smoke and mirrors."

"No, I mean it. You're pretty amazing."

Annie rolled her eyes and made a goofy face that she quickly regretted. Why couldn't she just take a compliment?

Finn turned, put his elbow on the back of the sofa, and rested his chin on his hand. "I've wondered why you never remarried."

Annie's heart leapt to her throat. "Oh. Well. I don't know."

"Did you even date?"

Annie paused as though she needed to think about it. "No."

"Not even once?"

"Not even." She shrugged as if it wasn't much of an issue.

He lowered his chin then looked up knowingly. "Annie."

She waited and hoped he would just let it go, but that stare of his was relentless. "Okay. The truth is, Ella was great, and I was okay. So why ruin a good thing? Bringing a man into our lives would've thrown off a delicate balance at best. At worst, well, I just didn't want to go there."

The look in Finn's eyes just about broke her heart. It was an odd mix of sympathy, grief, and buried pain.

"In some ways, our lives weren't all that different," Finn said. "We both lived for our kids and set our own needs aside. You know, sometimes, when we were here in the summers, I used to wonder—" He stopped abruptly and stood. "I'm a terrible host. Let me get you something to drink. What would you like? Soda? Coffee? Beer?"

Wonder what? She was willing to forego a drink to know what he'd been about to say, but he was already halfway to the kitchen, so she called out, "Water's fine." *Wonder what?*

When he returned with their drinks, Annie took a sip then set the glass on the coffee table. She blurted out, "Wonder what?"

The way he flinched made her worry he might spit out his soda. He set down his glass.

She repeated, "You said you used to wonder."

"Did I?" He looked up and slowly shook his head. "I don't remember. Must not have been very important."

"Finley Hilderman Burton, you're lying."

"You don't know that."

But she did. When he lied, he always glanced up and either ran his fingers through his hair or tapped his fingers on something. Of course, she wasn't about to reveal that to him.

He sank back and rested his head against the back of the sofa. "Okay. What about you? Have you ever wondered about us?"

"So you used to wonder about us?"

"I've said so, haven't I?"

"Well, no. You said that in Europe, you missed me. That's more of a homesick sort of thing—not an 'us' thing."

He gazed into her eyes then glanced away. He drew in a breath and exhaled. "You got married, then I did, and there wasn't an us. But there were times when we'd see each other from our separate yards, in our separate worlds. You looked very alone, and I felt very alone. At times like that, I wondered about us." Still leaning his head back, he stared at the ceiling.

Annie didn't know how to answer him. No, that wasn't true. She knew exactly how to answer him, but she was afraid to say it. The fact that he had been thinking of her while he was backpacking in Europe had been an enormous revelation, but this was even bigger. He'd kept on thinking about her and wondering about them. Her emotions were so close to the surface that with one word, the floodgates could open. That was all they needed right now—these feelings gushing all over the place. The potential flood damage alone would be appalling. But he looked so vulnerable. It all seemed so surreal.

Finally, she managed to speak. "The thing about being alone is it gets lonely. And you're inside your own head all the time. It makes it hard to keep things in perspective."

"Perspective?"

"Yeah?" *Perspective. Brilliant.*

His eyes narrowed as he turned and stared. "Now who's lying?"

She could not look away. She felt breathless and helpless to do anything but tell him the truth. "Okay, yes. I wondered."

There! Are you happy? Because I have a feeling you're about to break my heart all over again. So I hope you're pleased with yourself! But if that's what you wanted to hear, feel free to leap over to my side of the sofa and kiss me! Actually, I don't care if you wanted to hear it or not. Just catapult that toned body over here and plant your lips on mine.

Finn's lips parted. He looked stunned, confused, and a tiny bit terrified.

The door swung open, and Connor barged in. "I can't talk about it now. I'm going to bed."

Like two deer facing headlights, Finn and Annie

watched Connor storm past and climb up the ladder to his loft. Annie used to think the loft was so cozy and charming, but it was open to the downstairs. That meant they couldn't talk, which apparently wasn't a problem, since they seemed only able to stare at each other.

Annie stood. "I should go home."

Finn sprang to his feet. "I'll walk you home."

"That's okay."

"Remember that time the summer after sophomore year in high school when we found that bear pawing at the garage door?"

"Okay. Walk me home."

Finn grabbed his gun and holster from the gun safe, threw on a jacket, and turned on the outdoor floodlights, and they left.

Anything important they might've discussed was left back in the cabin. They talked about the weather and how little snow they'd had so far this winter. When they got to her door, Finn said, "Are we still on for shopping on Saturday?"

"Yes—provided Ella and Connor have worked things out by then."

Finn exhaled. "Couldn't we just put them in time-out while we're shopping?"

Annie laughed. "I'm not saying the concept doesn't have its merits, but probably not."

Finn shook his head and sighed. "That's a shame. I'll just pencil you in for Saturday."

"See you then."

As he walked away, he said, "Good night, Oakley."

11

Annie was somewhat relieved to have a day off from Finn. A little distance might help improve her perspective. The timing couldn't have been better. Ella and Connor weren't arguing anymore. In fact, they weren't talking at all. Annie couldn't have taken the radio silence, but Ella was stubborn.

Annie decided a little baking therapy might help shed light on the issue. They hadn't had a good heart-to-heart talk since Ella had arrived, so this was a perfect opportunity for it. Annie pulled a batch of brownies from the oven while Ella dropped cookie dough onto baking sheets.

Annie couldn't seem to find the right words for her question, so she just asked it. "What happened? I'm sorry if I'm prying, but I don't know how to help you."

Ella fixed her eyes on her mother for several long seconds. "You were right, okay?"

Annie was taken aback. "That's not why I was asking."

Ella sighed and glanced toward Finn's cabin. "I know. I'm sorry. I've got a short fuse lately."

That was a gross understatement, but Annie ignored it. "That's okay."

Ella put two cookie sheets into the oven and plopped down on a chair at the kitchen table. "Okay. We were at a Christmas party. He disappeared. I went looking for him. And I found him in the bedroom where the coats were laid out on the bed, tangled up in some woman's arms."

"They were in bed?"

"No! Sorry. I didn't explain that very well."

Annie sighed with relief then hoped she hadn't done it too loudly.

"They were standing inside the door."

"Maybe they were just talking." Even as she said it, Annie didn't feel convinced.

Ella stared knowingly.

Annie averted her eyes. What was there to say that would help? Since Ella and Connor had arrived, Annie assumed they'd been arguing about petty household things, the sort of things couples quibble over when they're really just having trouble adjusting to living together. But this was a whole other problem, one she couldn't solve.

Ella continued, "He might look like his father, but he's just like his mother."

Annie knew she was treading on dangerous ground, so she didn't say a word. Ella said, "His mother left Finn for somebody else. She had a wandering eye, and so does her son."

"You don't know that—about either of them. They were married for over two decades. She couldn't have wandered that much. It might just have been the one time." *Why am I defending Georgina?* "And it doesn't sound as though you've given Connor a chance to explain."

"Explain? Oh, I think I get it. People cheat."

Annie desperately wanted to find the right words, but what could she say? She didn't want to believe Connor would cheat, but denying the possibility wasn't fair to Ella either. "Okay, I'll admit that it doesn't look good."

Ella took a breath, but Annie continued before she could speak. "But what you saw could have a logical explanation."

Ella muttered, "Well, I'd like to know what it is."

Annie said gently, "You might try to give him the benefit of the doubt until you hear his side of the story."

"I heard enough, and I saw plenty. He'll just keep making excuses."

"Like what?"

"That she came on to him. Some nonsense about how he was just on his way to the bathroom when she appeared out of nowhere and threw herself at him. Like he wasn't strong enough to defend himself against a woman a foot shorter than he is?"

She understood how it must have made Ella feel, but the explanation sounded plausible to Annie. "Connor's a good-looking guy."

Ella pouted. "I know. He put in a lot of gym time in college. You should see his abs. They're amazing. And his shoulders. They're all muscly. I'll miss his shoulders." She appeared close to tears.

"So some woman found him attractive."

"I should have married a dumpy guy."

"Were they... kissing?" *Don't answer that. I don't think I want to know.*

"No, but she had her arms around him like some sort of evil octopus woman!"

"Look, I know I wasn't crazy about the idea of you two getting married."

"If you're going to say you told me so, I get it."

"No. I was going to say I know Connor. I've known him since he was a baby. I honestly think

Connor is one of the good guys, so maybe you should give him the benefit of the doubt."

Ella had the same wide-eyed, trusting look she had as a girl.

"What if some guy cornered you at a party. Wouldn't you want Connor to believe you?"

Reluctantly, she said, "Yeah, I guess."

Annie left out the part about how good people made mistakes too. Connor might be one of those guys. No one wants to think that the person they've fallen in love with could hurt them, but people did. How many women stayed in relationships with men who repeatedly hurt them? Annie would not let that happen to Ella. But before they went there, Ella needed the truth.

"How will I know if I can believe him—read his mind?" Ella asked.

"Maybe you could read his heart."

Ella leveled a condescending look at her mother. "Well, that's a very romantic notion, Mother, but life isn't like that, is it?"

"Maybe not always, but I'd like to believe there are people in this world we can trust."

"Like you trusted my father?" It wasn't like Ella to be this sarcastic.

"Trust wasn't the problem with Matt. He was just so caught up in his own life that he couldn't bring himself to come back down from those thrilling heights he loved climbing to. I think he forgot I was there on the ground." Annie was lost in the past for a moment. "But he was ecstatic about being a father. He adored you and couldn't wait to meet you."

Ella stared at the counter, deep in thought, then spoke softly. "Thanks, Mom."

"For what?"

"For you." She threw her arms around her mother's neck.

Annie hugged her. As she said a quick, silent prayer for her daughter, she lifted her chin and sniffed. "The cookies!"

She pulled the two smoking cookie sheets out of the oven, each of which contained a dozen evenly spaced charred discs. As Annie opened a window, she said, "If anyone deserves coal in their stocking, we've got it covered."

Connor followed Finn to the eighth tee. "Dad, nobody plays golf in December, at least not in upstate New York."

"They do if there's no snow on the ground."

"Look around. We're the only ones out here."

Finn stood tall and surveyed the landscape. "Fantastic, isn't it?"

Connor raised an eyebrow.

"Come on, where is your spirit of adventure?"

"I think it's frozen, along with my toes."

Finn clapped a hand on Connor's shoulder. "Man up, son!"

Connor turned a blank stare on his father. "Those parts are frozen too."

Finn suppressed a mischievous smile. Truth be told, he was chilled through. "How 'bout we finish the front nine and go grab a beer?"

"Yes!"

When they finished the ninth hole, Finn bent down to get his ball and stood up to find Connor had shouldered his bag and was on his way back to the car. It was Finn's turn to keep up with Connor. "The clubhouse is closed for the season."

Connor muttered, "Can't imagine why."

"So we can stop at the bar in the village."

"Sounds perfect." Finn was sure Connor would have found pretty much anything perfect by this point.

On the way back to town, they dissected their golf swings and putting techniques. By the time they took their seats at the bar, they were ready for a new topic, which Connor quickly supplied. "So, what's going on with you and Annie?"

Blindsided, Finn drew back. "Going on?"

"Oh, come on, Dad. It's obvious. You two have a vibe."

"A vibe?" Finn's mind raced. He couldn't just keep echoing Connor.

"Ella and I both picked up on it. It's okay. Mom has moved on. Now it's your turn."

"There's no vibe, and I don't need to move anywhere."

"I didn't mean literally." Connor looked a little surprised by his father's reaction. "I just meant you don't have to hide it from us."

All Finn could manage was a numb stare. If he didn't shut this down, it would only get worse. "I think it's nice that you and Ella have so much time on your hands to talk about us, but the more important question is, what's going on with you two?"

Connor clenched his jaw. "Ella is wrong, and she's stubborn."

Finn slowly nodded. "It's a good thing that you're not."

Connor stared at his beer. "You don't understand."

Finn narrowed his eyes. "You're right. How could

I possibly understand what it's like to be married?" He added under his breath, "For a week."

"Okay. Short version: She thinks I did something wrong. I did not. And she doesn't trust me."

Finn might have found it amusing if Connor weren't so clearly distraught. "Whatever it is, this issue isn't going anywhere unless you two talk."

Connor shook his head. "If she doesn't want to listen to my side of the story, then fine. It's a matter of pride."

"Pride has no place in a marriage." Finn was only half-joking. "Look, why don't you tell me what happened?" While Connor mulled it over, Finn ordered another round.

Connor stared at the bottles lined up on the bar then drew in a breath and began. "We were at my office Christmas party. I'm the new guy, so I had to go. I don't start until after the new year, but my boss thought this would give me a chance to meet everyone. I didn't really know anyone yet, so it was going to be awkward. We were just going to make an appearance then duck out and go have a holiday drink somewhere festive. We'd been there for maybe a half hour. We were actually having a good time. The people were nice. We even had some decent conversations, which doesn't always happen at that sort of thing. I was heading to the bathroom for a pit stop when a

woman I had chatted with for maybe two minutes
stopped me and asked if I knew where the coats were.

"I didn't even remember her name. I didn't care.
She looked a little unsteady, so I thought I should
help her and maybe call her a car share. She was in no
shape to drive. So if anything happened, I'd feel terrible. So we walked past a couple rooms, found the
coats piled on a bed, and we looked for hers. She
crawled onto the bed. I thought she was going to pass
out. By that time, I decided this was above my pay
grade, and I needed to get the hosts involved. I was on
my way to the door when she came up to me, grabbed
my necktie, and tried to pull me into her arms."
Connor glanced at his father. "I was pushing her
away when I saw Ella in the doorway."

Finn peered into Connor's eyes, searching for any
of the usual signs he was lying. Finn never had very
much reason to doubt his son, but sometimes, people
were tempted. People made mistakes.

Connor looked straight into his eyes. "Dad,
nothing happened."

Finn believed him. If Connor was lying, he
deserved some sort of acting award. But he'd seen his
son's fourth-grade play. Connor couldn't act this well.

Connor went on with his story. "Ella was upset,
obviously. But to her credit, she held it together and
made her apologies to the hosts. She said she wasn't

feeling well. Somewhere deep inside, she must have believed me a little, because she didn't just walk out. She found the hosts and told them she'd seen a young woman who looked like she'd had too much to drink. The couple hosting the party thanked her and said they'd take care of it. Ella graciously slipped her arm into mine, and we left.

"And she hasn't talked to me since."

Finn leaned back. "Well, that sucks."

"Thanks. I feel better already." There was no mistaking the sarcasm in his son's tone.

"Have you told this to Ella like you told it to me?"

"When I said she hasn't talked to me since, I guess what I really meant was she hasn't listened."

"When's the last time you tried?" Finn asked.

"The last time we were here."

"She's got to have calmed down a little."

"Yeah, but you know what? I don't care. She didn't trust me. And if she doesn't trust me, how can we build a life together?"

"I get that, but imagine how you'd feel if you were in her place."

"I'd trust her."

"Maybe you would, but it's not always easy. You're both new to this. This is hard for Ella. Marriage is hard."

"Thanks, Dad. I had no idea." He smirked.

Finn smiled. "Look, I've been there—well, not there with a bed full of coats—but every marriage has difficult situations. This won't be your last argument."

"Yes, it will, because I'm pretty sure my marriage is over."

"You'll get through this, and other arguments to follow, because you're in love and you made a commitment. And if both of those are true, you'll work it out."

"You make it sound like I have a choice. Tell all of that to Ella."

"Ella's hurting. And the only reason she's hurting so much is because she loves you so much." That seemed to make an impression. "Be the one to reach out and try again."

Connor looked unconvinced. "I'll think about it."

12

The next morning, Finn pulled onto the road with Annie beside him. Today was their big shopping day. With one week left until Christmas and a goal to finish all their shopping before the stores closed, they had their work cut out for them.

Annie glanced back toward their houses. "Do you think the kids will be all right?"

Finn laughed. "Are you thinking we should have called a sitter? 'Cause you just made it sound like they're ten."

"I was thinking more long-term, or at least till the end of the day."

Finn's grin faded. "If it were up to me, I'd lock the two of them in a room and not let them out till they figured it out. But it's not up to me."

Finn filled in Annie on Connor's side of the story.

"And you believe him?" Annie asked.

"If you'd asked me a year ago, I would have said absolutely, but after what his mother did... absolute trust isn't easy."

"That's a hard thing to deal with."

Finn said, "Trust is a fragile thing."

"I know." They were inching toward that uncomfortable zone, so Annie refocused. "I've veered off topic. We were talking about Ella and Connor."

"My fault. I'm the one who veered off course. I didn't mean to make it all about me."

"You didn't." He had never been selfish. That was one of the things that she loved about him. "So, fingers crossed, Ella and Connor will have a good talk today. And we'll come home to find them together again."

"I hope so. I can't believe Connor would hurt Ella like that. But convincing Ella..." His eyebrows drew together. "We might have to stop and see Santa today, 'cause I think it's going to take a Christmas miracle to bring those two back together."

"That's the hard part about being a parent. You can't put a Band-Aid on every wound."

Finn shook his head. "No, but I have faith in our kids. After all, they've got two brilliant parents."

Annie said, "You'd better be talking about the two in this car."

"I was hoping that was obvious." Finn's eyes sparkled. "Okay, it's game time. Gotta focus. If we're going to finish our shopping today, we have to have a firm plan and stick to it."

Annie had no idea what he was talking about. "Okay, coach. And your strategy is?"

"Shop till you drop."

"That is some strategic plan. I hope you didn't lose sleep over it."

"As it so happens, not a bit."

"Oh! I just remembered, when we get home, I have to find the ornaments. I've searched everywhere for them. They've got to be up there in that attic. If I don't find them, my tree will be naked." Her face went blank. "There is no tree. I don't have a tree."

"Now that you mention it, neither do I."

They looked at each other and both said, "Tomorrow."

Over lunch, Annie said, "I'm done."

Finn leaned back. "What? One morning of shopping has done you in?"

Now Annie felt guilty. "No. I mean I'm done shopping."

Finn slowly blinked.

She looked up and sighed. "Last night, while I watched Christmas movies, I did some—well, a lot—of my shopping online."

"Cheater."

"All the stores have sales and free-shipping deals. I couldn't resist."

Finn shook his head in disgust. "I should have laid out some ground rules earlier."

"On the plus side, there's less shopping to do."

"By which you mean now you'll help me? Thanks, Annie!"

She tried to act as though she didn't want to help, but the mischievous glimmer in his eyes made that almost impossible.

After lunch, Finn took Annie's hand and led her into a candy shop. Seeing her questioning look, he said, "Stocking stuffers."

"Does that mean Connor will be with you Christmas morning?"

"No. He decided to go to Vermont to spend Christmas with Georgina. But I'll be alone with one stocking that needs to be filled." He leaned closer, as if revealing a secret. "It's not Christmas without a chocolate Santa."

He bought two and dropped one in Annie's shopping bag. "Come on, Oakley, get with the program."

Once outside the store, Finn said, "That just about does it."

"Does what?"

"My shopping."

"What? But you said—"

"I was checking my email last night when I had a brilliant idea."

Annie's jaw dropped. "No fair! You made me feel guilty, when you shopped online too!" She tried to give him a playful shove in the shoulder, but he intercepted it and put an arm around her shoulder to immobilize her. It also rendered her helpless to the exhilaration of being so close. He released her, much to her disappointment, and they continued to the car. On the way, they passed the pond in the center of the village. Behind it, the village Christmas tree stood, lights twinkling. The gazebo was decked in red bows and greenery, with a red carpet leading to Santa and his elves. It was magical despite the lack of snow. But her inner child still loved a white Christmas.

Annie stopped to admire the scene. "Look at what we missed out on by only being here in the summer!"

He studied her with a look she'd seen before. Nothing good ever came from that look. He hooked his arm through hers. "Come on."

"What? Oh. No, I haven't skated in years."

"It's like riding a bike."

"No, Finn. Riding a bike is like riding a bike. This is like—"

"Fun? Yes, it is."

They were already halfway to the booth that rented out skates, and she didn't know how to say no. Well, that wasn't quite true. She knew how to say it. But Finn had never lost his youthful enthusiasm, and it was contagious. Soon, they were sitting on a bench and lacing up their skates. Annie watched skaters gliding carelessly along as though it were a perfectly natural thing to do. Finn took her hand and pulled her to her feet. As she hobbled along toward the ice, she tried to remember the last time she'd skated. She was pretty sure it had been in her single-digit-age era.

She proved Finn wrong. It wasn't like riding a bike. If Finn hadn't put a steadying arm around her waist, she would have fallen as soon as she stepped onto the ice. Instead, he more or less dragged her along as she unsteadily clung to him. Under any other circumstances, that would have made her ecstatic, but the fear of falling negated the thrill of their bodily contact.

"How are you doing this?" she asked.

"Doing what?" He looked blissfully unaware of her torment.

"Skating." Another near loss of balance

convinced her that simultaneously talking and skating was a lofty ambition.

"I play hockey with some guys a couple times a month."

Annie glared, much to Finn's amusement.

A couple of middle schoolers were racing each other when one brushed Annie as he passed and threw her off balance. Finn said, "Relax, Annie. I won't let you fall."

Then the kid's buddy zoomed past and bumped Finn on the opposite side. The next moment, Finn and Annie were both horizontal. While Annie sat up and brushed bits of ice from her sleeves, she muttered under her breath, "'Relax, Annie. I won't let you fall.'"

Something about her disgruntled state amused him as he quickly got up and helped Annie to her feet. After a concerted effort to suppress his broad grin and appear sympathetic, he asked, "Are you okay?"

"I will be once I make it to that bench over there." Once she was securely planted on the bench and unlacing her skates, she said, "I'm signing you up for a ballet class next week for revenge."

He laughed. "Come on, Annie, it wasn't that bad, was it?"

"The thing about skating as an adult is you've got so much farther to fall."

"But it's a fun kind of fall."

"Is it?" *Tell that to my tailbone.* Although, truth be told, it was almost worth the pain to have Finn's arm around her.

On the drive home, Annie gave in to her curiosity and texted Ella. *How are things with Connor?*

Her answer was a terse *Haven't seen him.*

She put her phone away and said, "Two days is a long time to go without talking."

Finn said, "I know it looked bad, but I've thought about it a lot. I don't believe Connor did anything wrong."

"How can you be so sure?"

"Because I know Connor. I'm pretty sure Ella would come around if she gave him another chance to explain, but he won't even try anymore. Ella's lack of trust hurt his pride."

Annie bristled. "Hold on. She told me what happened, and given the facts, her lack of trust was justified."

He lifted his palm in defense. "I didn't say that it wasn't. I said it looked bad, and it did. No one can fault Ella for her reaction. I'm just saying that Connor has a good explanation."

"Oops, I fell into my coworker's arms?"

"His overserved coworker made a pass at him, which he was resisting when Ella arrived. Annie, he loves her."

"Who, the coworker?"

"Ella! He loves Ella. Please don't make this worse!"

"Then why hasn't he tried to explain what really happened? He didn't even try to defend himself to her."

"He tried, but she wouldn't listen."

"She must've been really upset."

Finn said, "And understandably so. But when she wouldn't listen, he gave up trying. Now he's too proud to go begging—his words, not mine. And, as I said, he's hurt that she doesn't trust him."

Annie stared out the window. "That kind of trust must be hard so early on in a marriage."

"They'll figure it out."

"Will they?"

"If they want to stay married, they will."

Annie sighed. "I hope that's not too big an 'if.'"

The next morning, Annie climbed into Finn's SUV. "Go ahead. Ella's not coming with us."

"But we're going to a Christmas tree farm. I thought women love that sort of thing."

Annie frowned. "I'd like to point out what a sexist thing that was to say, except I do happen to love Christmas tree farms, so I'm not sure what to do about that."

"And what about Ella?"

"She loves Christmas tree farms too."

Finn blinked. "I meant, why isn't she coming?"

Now that question was simply ridiculous. "Because, as you well know, Connor left for skiing in Vermont early this morning. She's miserable about it."

Finn backed out of the driveway. "I think he gave up hope. You have to admit, he has tried for a week just to talk with her."

"I know. To be honest, I've never seen her like this. She just lies in bed all day, watching holiday movies and sleeping."

Finn drove down the road toward the Christmas tree farm. "Maybe with Connor gone, she'll snap out of it."

Annie couldn't believe he'd just said that. "I really don't think this is the sort of thing you just snap out of. It's the sort of thing that stays there until you talk it through."

Finn spoke in measured tones. "Which she refuses to do. Can you really blame him for choosing to go skiing in Vermont rather than standing outside her door and begging for an audience?"

"An audience?"

"That came out wrong."

"I'm not sure there's a way you could make that come out right."

Finn wrinkled his face. "Probably not."

His tone was so apologetic that she couldn't stay annoyed with him, especially when she agreed that Ella had been harsh not to hear Connor out. Of course, Annie wasn't about to admit that to Finn, lest it go to his head—or worse, lest it get back to Connor.

Finn said, "What I meant to say was sooner or later, they've got to figure this out for themselves."

"I know. You're preaching to the choir."

"So how 'bout we table this topic and focus on tree shopping?"

"Agreed."

13

As Finn pulled into a parking space in front of the tree farm, he felt lucky they'd found one at all.

Annie surveyed the field that served as a parking lot. "Looks like a few others had this idea before us."

"Come on, Oakley, we've got some hiking to do."

Once they'd made it through the barn and out the other side to the rows of Christmas trees, it took Finn less than five minutes to spot a small tree for his cabin. Twenty more minutes passed before Annie found hers. After leaving their trees to get shaken and baled, they grabbed two bowls of loaded-baked-potato soup and settled down at a picnic table near one of the outdoor propane heaters. Annie shivered.

Finn said, "You know, we could take these home, where it's warm."

She stared at him as though he'd lost his mind.

"Finn. Close your eyes. Breathe in slowly. What do you smell?"

At first, he thought it might be a trick question. "Pine trees?"

"Exactly! Now look around. What do you see?"

"Besides pine trees?"

She lifted her eyebrows.

"Lots of green stuff..." He watched for signs that he'd gotten the answer. "And lights... and decorations?"

"And?"

He knew there had to be an obvious answer, but he just couldn't come up with it. He was going to have to disappoint her. He offered an inadequate shrug.

She rolled her eyes. "Christmas magic!" She lifted her palms and said nothing, but her expression said, *Duh!*

Doing his best to be serious, Finn said, "You know, I was just about to say that."

"Of course you were."

He realized she was onto something when he glanced outside and saw about two dozen children and families lined up outside Santa's workshop while Christmas carols played throughout the area. In the other direction, a doorway led to a gift shop filled not only with gifts but ornaments and Christmas village buildings. "Annie!"

Alarmed, she asked, "What?"

"The ornaments! Did you find them?"

Her shoulders slumped. "I've been so focused on Ella, I completely forgot about those."

He took her hand and led her to the gift shop.

Apparently realizing where they were headed, she said, "Oh, Finn, that's okay. I know they're in the cottage somewhere. They'll turn up."

"Of course they will. My guess is sometime around Easter. I'm buying some ornaments and lights."

"But I've got more than enough for both of us."

"I'm sure you do." Ignoring her protest, he proceeded to fill a basket with ornaments and lights.

A voice from behind them said, "Sorry, sir, but we don't allow ornament hoarding."

They both reeled around to find Regi grinning. After holiday wishes and hugs, Regi said, "Would you mind if I stopped by tomorrow?" Her eyes sparkled. "I've got a couple items to drop off."

Annie said, "Sure! I'll cook dinner. Bring Derek. Finn, you'll join us, won't you?"

Before he could answer, Regi said, "Cooking dinner is too much trouble so close to Christmas."

Finn said, "I buy a mean pizza."

Annie considered. "That could work."

Regi's eyes lit up. "How can I turn down an offer like that?"

"You can't. How does seven sound?

"Seven it is. See you then." Regi headed out toward the trees while Finn and Annie went to load their own into the car.

Five hours later, Finn plopped down beside Annie on her sofa. "Whose idea was it to decorate both houses today?"

Ignoring his fatigue, she said, "I don't know, but it was a good one! Look around you."

Without lifting his head from the comfortable sofa, he surveyed the room. "It does look good, doesn't it?" So did she. "Merry Christmas, Annie."

As they sprawled side by side on the sofa, Finn was overwhelmed by a sudden desire to kiss Annie. So he quickly stood. "Well, it's been a long day. Don't get up." As he walked to the door, he said, "See you tomorrow."

Finn took long strides to his A-frame. *What was that?* It wasn't even the first time that day he'd thought about kissing Annie. Since they'd found themselves back at Cedar Creek, emotions he'd tamped down years before had come flooding back. Everyone told him—whether he asked them or not— that he'd be too vulnerable for any serious relationship for at least a year after his divorce. But dating hadn't even occurred to him until now.

Finn walked inside and got a fire going in the wood stove. Since spending time with Annie again, he'd found himself wanting more. Doing something about it, however, took him back to that moment over two decades ago. If Annie had ever had those sorts of feelings for him, she wouldn't have run off and married Matt. That alone was a sign that Finn wasn't her type. There could be no more polar opposite of Finn than Matt.

Even if she had any interest in him, shifting gears from friendship to romance was too risky. How many dating relationships lasted a lifetime? Not many. If things didn't work out, their friendship—if it even survived—would never be the same. The thought of losing Annie was too much to bear.

What did I say? Annie stared at the door Finn had just closed. Everything had been fine all day between them. They'd had fun decorating his house then hers. He hadn't seemed like he was in that much of a hurry when they went up to the attic to search for the ornament box. Annie told him she'd be fine using the ornaments they'd bought at the Christmas tree farm, but he insisted. It took half an hour, but they found it. She recalled his expression when she saw it and turned to him. He was so happy for her.

Had she done something to reveal her deeper feelings for him? After all these years, had she suddenly slipped up and scared him away? Even so, how could he rush out like that without saying something? She knew the answer. What could he say? "I'm sorry I don't love you back?" There were no words that wouldn't make it worse. In his place, she might do the same. Just walk away. Maybe run.

14

After his hasty departure the evening before, Annie wasn't sure whether Finn would still come to the pizza party. So when he knocked at the door, she was relieved but a little uneasy. Still, if she'd done something wrong, wouldn't she have an inkling of what it could be? But in he walked, carrying three pizza boxes and a twelve-pack of beer. He went straight to the fridge with the beer then turned and drew in a breath as though he were about to say something. Ella walked in, and whatever it was remained unsaid.

Finn had said hello, and although Annie had said hello back, there was unvoiced tension between them. Annie couldn't blame either of them. While it wasn't Finn's fault, his son had just left Ella alone with unresolved issues between them. As far as she was concerned, Finn was on Team Connor.

Annie chimed in with news of the weather. A nor'easter was brewing and heading their way in the next couple of days. "I don't know about you, but I'm ready for snow. I like it for Christmas and New Year's, and then it can stop. Of course, it never does."

Finn and Ella smiled politely. Ella's eyes darted anywhere but in Finn's direction. "The decorations look great. It's very festive and Christmassy in here." Ella smiled, but it didn't reach her eyes. At least she was making an effort.

A door knock put them out of their misery. It was Regi with a stranger in tow.

"Annie, this is Alex Laghari. Derek had to work, so I brought Alex. He's new in town, so I thought I'd introduce him to some of the locals."

Regi's friend Alex wouldn't be friendless for long. He was staggeringly good-looking. Annie tried not to stare as she took in his dark eyes, strong cheekbones, regal nose, and black tousled hair. As he walked in and met Ella and Finn, Annie turned to Regi with a wide-eyed, questioning look.

Regi said to the others, "We'll be right back." She turned to Annie. "I've got to see that dress you were telling me about." She dragged a confused Annie to the bedroom and said in hushed tones, "You're welcome. I tried to tell you Alex is hot—and he just bought your dream house. You're meant for each other."

"Except for the part where I told you I'm not looking for a relationship right now."

"Well, it found you. As much fun as it must be to live the life of a cloistered nun in the woods, this is a real opportunity."

"You make it sound like a business investment."

"Well, honey, if I were single, I'd want that asset in my portfolio."

Annie's mouth hung open for a moment. "I'm just not ready."

Regi gave her a no-nonsense look. "Well, get ready, 'cause you deserve to be happy."

Annie didn't feel at all happy at the moment. "Does he know why you've brought him here?"

"I brought him to make some new friends. That's all."

Annie exhaled. "We'll talk later."

Annie walked into the kitchen to find Finn playing host while Ella set out plates and napkins. Alex stood with his back to her, looking tall and broad shouldered. Hearing Annie and Regi approaching, he turned and flashed an engaging smile. She couldn't fault her friend's taste. Anyone with a pulse would find this guy attractive.

Her musings were interrupted when Ella peeked

into the first pizza box then discreetly went over to Annie and whispered, "Sorry, Mom. I'm not feeling well." She escaped to her room while Annie made apologies for her.

As the evening went on, Annie gave up trying to find Alex's flaw. Everyone had at least one. If she could find his, she'd have an excuse to offer Regi so her friend would let go of this dating idea. But Alex was charming and smart. He'd even brought her a gift, which was entirely unnecessary, since Regi had brought not only a hostess gift but a Christmas gift too.

After dinner, they casually sat around the fireplace. What began as stories of favorite past Christmases evolved to reminiscing about past Cedar Creek summers.

Finn had just finished telling how they could identify every summer until about age thirteen by which play-related injury one or both of them had sustained.

Annie said, "My favorite was the tire swing."

Finn winced. "Age twelve."

Annie tried to pout, but her laughter won out. "There was this tire swing hanging from a branch over the creek. All the kids used to do it. We'd jump on the tire and swing out over the creek. Well, Finn's turn came, and the rope broke."

"Everyone was laughing too hard to see I was hurt —except Annie."

Annie shook her head as if it was nothing.

Finn said, "Doctor Annie made a splint with some sticks and a beach towel and walked me home. I had a cast on my arm for the rest of the summer."

Alex smiled at Annie. "So, how long have you two been married?"

Annie froze, glanced at Finn, and caught Regi's stunned expression from her peripheral vision. "Oh! No! We're not...!" She realized she had pointed to Finn and herself at least twice. Then she laughed a weird, uneasy laugh. "We're not married! We're friends." She laughed again and said, "Yeah, we're just friends." By the time she made something akin to an umpire's gesture for safe, Finn had the most peculiar expression. She couldn't quite pinpoint its meaning, but he wasn't amused. That much she knew.

Alex, on the other hand, looked thoroughly charmed. So she smiled at him. Their eyes locked for a moment.

Regi came to the rescue and brought everyone back to some semblance of normalcy. "How about a game of charades?" She said it with such enthusiasm that everyone agreed. Regi assigned teams, claiming Finn for herself, which left Annie and Alex together.

An hour later, it was down to the wire. Both

teams were tied. It was Annie's turn to pantomime. It was a movie. Two words. Annie mimed pulling something over her shoulders. Everyone called out their answers.

Finn said, "Sweater!"

Regi called out, "Coat!"

Alex said, "Shawl. *Shawshank Redemption!*"

Alex leaped up. They both cheered and then hugged. Still feeling victorious, Annie turned, smiling, to Finn. He appeared oddly stunned. The air was electric. No one moved until Regi's eyes darted from Annie to Finn, and she quickly got up and congratulated Alex.

Annie said, "I can't remember the last time we did this."

Finn appeared to be trying to climb out of the dark place he'd fallen into. "It was your broken-toe summer. One afternoon, it was raining. I came over to check up on you. You'd finished your book, and you begged me to play charades."

"Oh, that's right. I remember." The rest of the memory came back to her. "You hated charades."

He nodded with a pointed look that left no doubt that hadn't changed.

"Finn, I'm sorry. I completely forgot."

He shrugged and smirked as though it didn't really matter, but it obviously did. Still, not liking a game didn't seem like a good enough reason to brood for the entire evening. Something else had to be going on. Maybe he was upset about Connor spending Christmas with Georgina. Whatever it was, she couldn't do anything about it at the moment.

Regi said, "Well, I hate to be the one to say it, but I've got work tomorrow."

Finn excused himself and disappeared down the hall.

Regi said, "Tell Ella we missed her. I hope she feels better."

Annie wished she and Regi could talk more about Ella. She worried her daughter had taken this argument with Connor so much to heart that it was affecting her health. But Alex was there, so she nodded and said she'd pass along Regi's thoughts.

While Alex helped Regi with her coat, Annie studied him. He had a presence that was undeniable. And those dark eyes of his could give a weaker woman a case of Victorian vapors, but Annie was strong. Still, she found herself recalling how her shoulders had landed just below his when they'd embraced. It was a sturdy embrace. If she were to pass out from the vapors, he would catch her brilliantly.

Finn cleared his throat, giving Annie a start.

She'd been staring at Alex and hadn't heard him arrive at her side. "Oh! I'll get your jacket."

"Got it."

Sure enough, he was wearing it. "Oh."

Alex reached out to shake Annie's hand. "Thank you so much. I've enjoyed meeting you."

"Same here. I hope you like Cedar Creek. It's a nice community."

Regi gave her a hug. There were jovial Christmas wishes all around, then the two made their way through the door.

Finn said, "Good night, Annie."

Annie smiled. "Good night. Thanks again for the pizza."

Finn lifted his chin in a half nod and left.

She had never thought about it before, but Finn usually stayed behind to clean up and chat about how the evening had gone. There wasn't much to do now except put the leftover pizza in the fridge, but she missed their debriefing. She went to check on Ella and heard her snore softly, something she always insisted that she didn't do. Ella sounded fine.

It was Finn she was worried about.

15

We need to talk. That was the cryptic message that had popped up on Annie's phone no more than an hour after everyone left the previous night.

Regi, you just left my house, Annie texted.

But we couldn't talk then. Are you free for breakfast at nine?

Annie had envisioned sleeping in until ten but let go of that dream. *Sure.*

Great. Diner breakfast at nine.

See you then.

Annie set down her phone with a curious frown. There was something almost cloak-and-dagger about Regi's vague message. She had to have known Annie would stew about this all evening.

As it turned out, Annie didn't stew for long. She picked up a book from the stack on her nightstand

and started to read. When her watch alarm went off at eight thirty, she awoke with her face resting on the open book. If pillow face was a thing, Annie had book face.

She walked into the bathroom, half expecting to look in the mirror and see the reverse of page forty-seven imprinted on her left cheek. One look at her face made her wonder if that wouldn't have been an improvement. She solved the problem by averting her eyes. She pulled on some jeans and a sweater, ran a brush through her hair, brushed her teeth, and headed out the door. At 8:59 a.m., Annie slipped into a booth where Regi and a hot cup of coffee were waiting for her.

"I've got a meeting in an hour with the contractor for the second salon," Regi said.

Annie leaned forward. "That's so exciting!"

Regi was beaming. "It is. But that's not why we're here." She raised an eyebrow and quietly said, "He likes you."

Annie didn't know how to react. "You don't mean Finn, do you?"

Regi shook her head knowingly.

Annie couldn't deny she found Alex attractive, but it was more of an admiring-from-afar sort of attractive—like a movie star. Sure, they looked good on the big screen, but who'd want to date one? Those guys were so out of touch with the real world, she couldn't imagine a conversation with one. But Alex Laghari? She'd spent enough time with him to imagine he could never be boring. And he was kind.

Regi waved her hand before Annie's glazed-over eyes. "Annie? You went somewhere just now—I'm assuming with Alex?" She made a crooked face that, under any other circumstances, would have made Annie laugh.

Instead, Annie felt herself blush. "Regi, you're—"

"Right?"

"Crazy! I'm not dating Alex!"

"Not yet."

Panic was setting in quickly. "I can't."

"Why not?"

"Well, for one thing, it's been over two decades since I've gone on a date!"

Regi smiled. "You're right. Let's not rush things."

Annie narrowed her eyes. "Very funny."

Regi lowered her chin and looked over her glasses. "Why won't you let yourself be happy?"

I don't know. But she did know. She just couldn't say it out loud.

Regi's eyes softened. "Annie, honey, Finn's a great guy, but you can't carry that torch for the rest of your life."

Why not?

"Because if you hold a torch long enough, it eventually burns you." Regi tried another tack. "Give me one good reason why you can't go out with Alex."

"He's too handsome."

"Yeah, that would suck—having to look at that face all the time! But because you're not shallow, you would see past his perfectly proportioned features to what a nice guy he is. He really is, Annie."

"I know your business is really taking off, but have you ever thought of selling used cars?"

Regi leaned back and folded her arms with a scowl.

"'Cause this is a really hard sell."

"Because he's perfect for you. He's easy to look at. I guess we've established that fact. He's nice and successful, and he just bought your dream house. What more could you want?"

"Love?" It made Annie sad to admit it, knowing how unlikely it was.

Regi exhaled. "You don't know that you won't fall in love with him."

"And I don't know that I will."

"No one ever does! That's what dating is for!"

"Aren't you leaving something out?" Annie asked. "He hasn't asked me out."

Regi closed her eyes and shook her head. "Because asking you last night would have been awkward. I was there. Finn was being weird. Who wants to ask someone on a first date in front of an audience? That's why he asked me about you on the way home. He didn't want to be pushy or make it awkward for you, so he gave me this." She handed Annie a business card with a handwritten message on the back.

Coffee sometime? His phone number followed.

Annie stared at the card for a moment. "It's pretty cryptic."

Regi's eyes widened. "It's a business card, Annie, not an illuminated manuscript."

Annie tore her eyes from the note and looked up at her friend. This couldn't be happening.

Regi nodded. "Call him."

"I'll think about it."

"Don't think too long." Regi glanced at her watch. "I've got to go." She squeezed Annie's hand. "You can do it." She stopped by the register to pay and walked out of the diner, leaving Annie still studying the card.

Two hours later, Annie sat at her kitchen table with the card in her hand and her cell phone on the table. She'd already started to dial twice and lost her courage. But Regi was right. It was time to let go of her feelings for

Finn. Guys like Alex didn't stumble into her life every day. She was making too much out of this. It was only a date—not even that. It was coffee. Even if it didn't work out, he could turn out to be a good friend. Annie's shoulders slumped. *Just what I need—another guy friend I'm attracted to. Am I attracted to Alex? He's attractive. And he's nice. And fun. He's a kick-ass charades player. What if we could be a thing?* She sighed. *Well, you're not going to find out if you don't call him.*

Ella wandered into the kitchen, drying her hair from a shower.

Annie hastily slid the card under the napkin holder. "Feeling better?"

Before Ella could answer, a loud knock on the door startled them both. Finn yelled, "Annie! Open the door!" She was still opening it when he said, "It's Connor. He's had a ski accident."

Annie shoved her phone into her purse and, leaving the card on the table, threw some clothes in a bag and rushed out to the car. While Ella zipped up her suitcase and followed, Annie dashed off a quick text to Regi, asking her to check in on Mr. Willoughby while they were gone.

Annie insisted on driving the three-hour trip to Stowe. While she drove, Finn and Ella passed along regular updates from Georgina's texts. Connor had swerved to miss another skier then lost control and gone into the trees. Georgina and Adam were skiing with him when it happened. "He's conscious."

Ella said, "That's a good sign, isn't it?"

Finn nodded. "They'll know more after a CAT scan and an MRI."

Ella set her phone in the armrest pocket. "I should have talked to him before he left." She stared out the window with tears in her eyes.

Finn glanced back at her. "He was too stubborn to tell you again that he didn't do anything wrong."

That tipped Ella over the edge. Tears trailed down her cheeks. "He should have told me again."

"I'm not saying he was right, but he thought you should've trusted him no matter what."

Ella dug through her purse and pulled out a crumpled tissue. "That's a pretty tall order, don't you think?"

Finn said, "I think he loves you, and you love him."

Ella nodded as she blew her nose and wiped the tears from her face.

Annie glanced at her daughter in the rearview mirror. "It'll be okay."

That brought on a new surge of tears. "You always say that."

Their phones dinged, and Finn read his text. "It's not life-threatening."

Ella stared through her tears at her phone then gave up and set it down. Looking relieved, she laid her head back on the car seat. "What else?"

"That's all for now."

Finn put down his phone and stared straight ahead at the road. Annie could see he was worried, but she suspected he was trying not to reveal it to Ella. Annie reached over and gave Finn's hand a squeeze. He held on to her hand for a moment then released it. From the sniffles and snorts in the back seat, it was clear that Ella was falling apart—not that Annie could blame her. But Ella had always been calm in emergencies. Annie reminded herself that Ella had never been through anything like this. This was her husband.

Annie set aside her worries and forced herself to focus on driving. The best thing she could do for Ella and Finn was to get them safely to Connor.

After a miserably long three hours, they pulled into the hospital parking lot. Georgina's fiancé, Adam, met them at the entrance, looking like the sort of guy who did men's outdoor-magazine underwear ads, complete with a smug, crooked smile. He and Finn managed to ignore the awkwardness of the situation while Adam brought them all up to speed. Georgina couldn't leave Connor's side. He had just come back from a CAT scan and an MRI and was back in his room. Adam would take them there now.

Ella whispered to Annie, "What if he doesn't want me there? Should I wait outside? But I want to be with him. I don't know what to do."

Annie assured her, "He needs you."

"But what if he doesn't want me there... ever?"

Annie paused outside the hospital room and took Ella's hands in hers. "Do you love him?"

"Yes, of course I love him!"

"Then love him. Be there for him."

Despite her obvious distress, Ella nodded, took a deep breath, and went inside.

Georgina turned and watched Ella come into the room, but she made no effort to move.

Ella rushed to the opposite side of the bed. "Connor!" Ella took his hand then froze. "I'm sorry. Does that hurt?"

He smiled. "No, my hand's fine, but my head's pounding."

The doctor walked in, still reading Connor's chart. "There's a good reason for that." She glanced around at the others.

Connor said, "Go ahead. They're all family."

"I'm afraid the tree was harder than your head. You've fractured your skull." The doctor set down the chart and pulled out a small flashlight. "Let's take a look." She examined his eyes, checked the goose egg on his head, then checked his strength and reflexes. She picked up Connor's chart. "Luckily, no brain bleed or damage. But you have a good scalp hematoma, which is some superficial bleeding over your skull. It's a slight crack that should resolve on its own. You can thank your helmet for that."

Connor looked up at the doctor. "So what now?"

"There's no surgery indicated at this point. The pain should subside in five to ten days, but the healing process can take months. So no contact sports for a month. That includes Christmas shopping. No brawling in the store aisles over TVs. And no sports of any kind until you've seen your doctor at home. Any questions?"

"No, got it."

"We're keeping you overnight for observation, then we're sending you home tomorrow whether you like it or not." She grinned, wished them happy holidays, and left.

Ella returned to his side. "Connor, I love you."

"Does this mean you forgive me?"

She answered with teary eyes. "Yes."

"Will I always have to be hospitalized before you'll forgive me?"

"It depends." A smile bloomed on her face.

Everyone gathered round and chatted until Connor yawned. "Sorry, guys. I'm really tired."

Finn said, "We'll let you get some rest. Ella, why don't you keep an eye on Connor while we step outside?"

In the hallway, they stood in a clump and conversed with polite restraint about Connor. When they got to the weather, Annie turned to Finn. "We should go get checked into the hotel." *The hotel that we haven't booked.* Panic struck as she thought of the hotels being full. She could only imagine having to stay at Georgina's—Finn, his ex-wife, her future husband, Ella, and Annie—all together under one roof. Before she did that, she would carve out a bed in a snowbank amid the throes of a raging blizzard until snotsicles hung from her nostrils like Doctor Zhivago.

That was when Georgina proved that she wasn't all bad by having the good taste to be silent.

It was Finn himself who actually made things just a little more awkward by taking so long to pick up on Annie's cue. "Our hotel? Right. Can't miss check-in. Better go. We'll see you around." He ducked his head into the hospital room. "We're going out for a bit. We'll bring you back something to eat."

As they slid into their car seats, Annie said, "Thank God."

She hoped Finn would assume she meant Connor's prognosis, but as she booked a nearby hotel on her phone, she was almost as thankful for avoiding a visit with Georgina and Adam. Five minutes later, they checked into their rooms and headed for a restaurant one of the nurses had recommended. As they followed the hostess, they turned a corner, and there, smiling over their menus, were Georgina and Adam.

Finn couldn't think of a way not to join them.

The next morning, after having endured enough small talk with Georgina to last a lifetime, Finn stood in Connor's room with the rest of their group, waiting for Connor to be discharged. By this point, they'd practically resorted to saying random words to avoid awkward silences. Connor was repeating his treatment instructions to Georgina when he got to the part about no contact sports for six months.

Ella said, "Is childbirth considered a contact sport?" That got everyone's attention. Her eyes shone as she exchanged glances with Connor then smiled at the others. "While Connor was having some tests, I grabbed a test of my own at the hospital pharmacy."

Georgina gasped and clutched Adam's shoulder

while Ella turned to her mother and shrugged. "Turns out I am pregnant, after all."

Annie gave Ella a long hug. For the first time since they'd all arrived, they were all far too ecstatic to be awkward.

16

It was close to noon by the time Connor was discharged from the hospital, so Georgina insisted they all go to her place for a celebratory lunch. Connor's positive outcome seemed to enable everyone to ignore any tension that might lie under the surface, as well as Georgina's enormous engagement ring—or at least they tried. In truth, no one could ignore something like that, especially when Georgina took every opportunity to gesticulate wildly with her left hand. Once, Annie overheard Finn mutter to himself, "That's a statement." Other than that, everyone was impressive in their restraint.

As soon as they were able, Finn and Annie headed for home, leaving Connor and Ella with Georgina for Christmas as planned. By late afternoon, Christmas lights decking houses and storefronts were beginning to twinkle. Every village they drove through seemed to have come to life from a storybook, sporting festive town squares, enchanting lighted gazebos, and sparkling Christmas trees that shimmered in the night sky.

It was Finn's turn to drive, so Annie leaned back and enjoyed the ride home. She felt blessed to be able to take in the sights, knowing that a ski accident that could have ended in tragedy instead would end with Connor's full recovery. *And a grandchild.* Annie paused and drew in a breath. *I'm going to be a grandmother.* That filled her thoughts for a number of miles.

After riding along lost in thought, Annie realized she and Finn had barely spoken a word. Granted, driving Vermont country roads at dusk did command his attention, but this was a little beyond what was required. She wondered if his pizza-party mood had come back and wedged itself between them. Unable to stand the silence any longer, Annie pulled out her earphones and listened to an audiobook for the remaining two hours.

It was dark when Finn pulled into the driveway. As they got out of the car, Finn said enough to be civil, then they went their separate ways. The cottage was cold, so that kept Annie busy turning up the heat and starting a fire. Mr. Willoughby was happy to see her. That and the Christmas lights lifted her spirits as she made some hot chocolate and settled down by the fire. She picked up a book, took a sip of hot cocoa, and read. But thoughts of Finn ruined her concentration until she gave up trying to read. With a sigh, she got up and pulled *Six Weeks* from her Christmas movie collection and wept over Dudley Moore's exquisite score.

Then she wept over Finn. *How long should it take to fall out of love? Couldn't love just expire then vanish along with the pain?*

Annie woke up on the sofa with an array of crumpled tissue scattered about. *Well, that was productive.* She hadn't stayed up late crying over Finn in a very long time. She tried to blame it on the stress of the past few days, but she knew that wasn't it. Here she thought she'd done such a good job of relegating what they had to friendship. But when he shut her out with no explanation, she was devastated. Relationships had breakups, but friends simply drifted apart with no explanation required.

Annie stood. *I am not going to spend Christmas like this.* She had the perfect opportunity to have the Christmas of her dreams, and she was determined to make it happen. For starters, she'd have a leisurely coffee.

The first thing she saw on the way to make coffee was Alex's card peeking out from beneath the napkin holder. She slid it from its hiding place then stared as though it were toxic and could not be touched. She turned away and made coffee without looking back.

With Christmas two days away, this was the perfect time to do some last-minute housecleaning—not that anyone would see it. She would be completely alone. She and Finn had talked about spending Christmas together, but those plans were obviously off. Still, a light cleaning served two purposes. It would keep her mind off Finn, and the house would be perfect for Christmas. She convinced herself there was something appealing about being alone in a spotless house. She could do what she wanted and create her own Christmas magic with books, movies, music, and food. She would make all her holiday favorites and wear fuzzy socks and flannel pajamas all week.

She finished cleaning everywhere else and arrived in the kitchen. A quick wipe down and mopping was all it needed. But then she spied the business card sitting where she'd left it.

She finally broke down and picked up the card. *Alex Laghari.* When she'd stared at it and wondered long enough, she exhaled and opened the junk drawer. Something stopped her. *So what if we have coffee? It wouldn't be like a date. It would be more of a practice date. And he was really nice—and interesting. It wouldn't have to be anything more.*

But thinking and doing were two separate things. *Maybe later.* She got her purse from the hook by the door and tucked the card inside her wallet. It could wait. It was too close to Christmas, and people had plans. If she did call, she would do it after Christmas —after the new year was better.

She became engrossed in her recipe files and spent an hour compiling a shopping list. It was helping. She felt better already. With the exception of one stolen glance toward Finn's cabin on her way to the car, she managed to focus on her objective—creating her ideal Christmas.

The village of Cedar Creek was humming with holiday energy. The Dickensian Christmas festival of the previous weekend was over, but the charming Victorian shop stalls remained. There wasn't a window on Main Street that wasn't framed in fresh evergreen garlands. The sight lifted her spirits. This was going to be a magical Christmas. She would have complete control of her environment. No one would be there to bring down the room or to ski into a tree. For her, Christmas was going to be all about twinkling lights, delectable treats, and scented candles. She'd get into bed, fluff up her six pillows, and lean back and read while snow gently drifted down outside her window.

Still caught up in her holiday daydream, she was about to go into the bakery to stock up on her favorite holiday treats when she heard someone calling her name. She turned to find Alex heading her way from the shop next door.

He said, "I just walked out of the hardware store and saw you. I decided it had to be fate."

Annie smiled. He was indeed charming, and she hadn't been charmed in years. "So, how are you settling into your new house?"

"Very well." He lifted his bag from the hardware store. "Picture hangers. There's a lot to be done, but I'll get there."

"It takes time, especially with a vacation home when you're not there all the time."

"Oh, no, this is my full-time home now. I've taken a small apartment in Albany for when I have work there, but most of my work can be done by remote, so Cedar Creek is home now."

Annie smiled then feared she looked a little too pleased by the news. "Well, that's nice. I hope you'll like it here."

"I'm sure I will." His smile faded, but his gaze

lingered. He hesitated then asked, "Do you have time for a coffee?" He glanced inside the bakery. "That table by the window looks awfully inviting."

"Sure." As they went in and sat down by the window, Annie felt thoroughly content. There was something so wonderfully self-indulgent about sitting at midday in a coffee shop with nothing pressing to do. Doing so with a fascinating man made it even more so.

Alex was easy to talk to and even easier to listen to. He had an engaging manner that made her feel comfortable. She was bringing him up to date on her life story, culminating with Connor's ski accident, when the church bell chimed on the hour. She glanced at her watch. "I'm so sorry! I didn't mean to take up so much of your time."

"Not at all. I've enjoyed it."

She believed him. "Me too." She tore herself from his gaze. "I'll let you get on with your life, and I've got some grocery shopping to do."

Alex insisted on paying the check. Without thinking of what she was saying, Annie said, "I'll get it next time." *Next time?*

They parted ways outside the shop, leaving Annie deep in thought as she wandered up and down the grocery store aisles. *What is this? Could it turn into something?*

Her phone dinged, and her heart leaped. Then she remembered Alex didn't have her number. That was why she sucked at dating. A savvy woman would've found a way to slip that to him. The only one with the phone number was Annie, which put the ball back in her court. When she finally dug her phone out of her purse, it was only the utility company warning of the oncoming storm. She'd been so caught up in the trip to Vermont and Connor's accident that she hadn't paid much attention to the news or weather. She was thrilled to read it was going to snow. There had hardly been any snow this season. All the ski resorts had relied on their own man-made snow. But now, snow was coming. She would have her white Christmas.

Finn had a few errands to run before he settled in for the holiday weekend. At the top of the list was stock-piling a week's worth of food. He loaded his cart with frozen pizzas, hot dogs, hamburger patties, and spaghetti, then he walked out to his car. He was reminding himself to get fuel for the generator when he glanced at the bakery window and saw Annie and Alex Laghari looking starry-eyed at each other over coffee.

It wasn't enough that I had to spend two days with Georgina and Adam—now this!

Annie started to turn toward him, so he lifted a grocery bag in front of his face, and he walked past the bakery to his car.

Alex didn't waste any time. And what about her? Miss I-don't-want-to-be-in-a-relationship-so-I'll-stay-single-for-two-decades-to-prove-it! Years of independence tossed away in an instant. And for what? A pretty face! He'd thought Annie was deeper than that. It would be different if she'd known Alex—maybe even for years—and knew what she was getting into. But this was just reckless behavior.

Finn thought he and Annie had grown closer since they'd both moved back to Cedar Creek. But now things were different. He felt different. Maybe he even had feelings for her. It was too early to tell. And he had just gotten divorced. The last thing he wanted was to jump off a cliff into a relationship. No one could blame him for that. So he'd assumed he and Annie had time. Apparently, Annie didn't want time. She wanted that disgustingly good-looking guy.

This is ridiculous. Didn't you learn your lesson from going through this the first time? No, that was different. I was in love—or so I thought. But how could it have been love with Annie when I'd just come back from a summer in Europe with my girlfriend?

The thing was, she was Annie. She'd always been that—his best friend. They were there for each other. That was what made it so good. All those feelings of love were just roadblocks between them, keeping them from being... what they were.

Lately, he'd wondered what it would take to capture Annie's heart. He'd given it a lot of thought— too much thought. She was too smart and independent to do something impulsive. Like marry Matt on a whim? But she had already made that mistake, which was why it would take a miracle to bring her to the altar.

Whoa! Hold on a minute! Nobody said anything about marriage! Let's just take a step back and regroup.

He was way overanalyzing this. Seeing her there in the bakery drinking in coffee and that guy's lingering gaze made it clear that he'd overestimated her. If he had fully examined the history, he would have remembered her type. She'd married Matt. She'd even admitted that she had been dazzled by him. Dazzled! Alex wasn't wild like Matt, but he was the kind of guy who walked into a room and got noticed.

Annie liked flashy guys. Finn would never be flashy. He would always be the boy next door, no one special, just a guy she hung out with when nobody else was around.

He couldn't understand why this bothered him so. He was almost behaving like she'd been unfaithful to him, but they'd never been close to romantic. In fact, the idea of dating Annie seemed absurd at this point. It would be like starting over forty-three years after they'd begun. Except they had never begun.

Instead, what they had was an unspoken agreement to be there for each other, or so Finn had assumed. His heart sank.

That was just a fairy tale I made up in my head, when the truth is, Annie wants a man in her life. And that man is Alex.

So that was settled. All Finn needed to do was get over it.

Did she even know anything about Alex? Finn hadn't been able to get much out of him in the way of background except that he was a lawyer and partner in an Albany lobbying firm. That sounded shifty. He was a new friend of Regi's. But she could be flaky at times. She was the type to pull over and pick up a stray if it looked lost. Usually, that meant dogs and cats, but this time, it was Alex. He was Regi's rescue guy.

What if Annie needed to be rescued from Alex?

17

Annie unpacked the groceries and got to work baking. It wasn't a proper Christmas without Christmas cookies. While her favorite Christmas playlist played carols, she measured and stirred her way to three batches of cookies—sugar cookies in holiday shapes, Scottish shortbreads, and classic chocolate chip. The whole cottage smelled like heaven, assuming heaven smelled like brown sugar, butter, and hot chocolate simmering on the back burner. And why wouldn't it? Could there be a more heavenly smell?

Her original plan had been to make cookies and then make a casserole for dinner, but after cleaning up her baking mess, she decided a sandwich would be good enough. After all, this was her perfect Christmas. No one expected anything from her. She could do whatever she wanted. Right now, she wanted to put her feet up. Night had fallen, so she did her usual outside inspection to make sure the car was inside the garage with the door shut. Only then did she realize it was snowing. Big, fluffy flakes had already blanketed the ground. She drew in a deep breath. Her Christmas alone just got better and better.

She ran out of firewood but decided to read one chapter from her book before going out to the woodpile. She warmed up the hot chocolate she'd made earlier and put two cookies on one of her grandmother's bone-china dessert plates then cozied up with a fluffy throw blanket on the sofa and Mr. Willoughby at her feet. Annie decided she was fully on board with the whole concept of Christmas vacation.

Halfway through her chapter, the cottage went dark. She'd lost power. Using her phone's flashlight, she found some candles and a lighter and was about to light them when she remembered that she was out of wood. She couldn't leave lit candles with a cat in the house, so she saved the task for later. After three trips to the woodpile, she had a neat stack of wood outside the door and enough wood inside by the fireplace to last until morning. She'd just settled down by the fire with an extra blanket and her book when her phone rang. Caller ID lit up the screen.

She took a breath and answered the call. "Finn?"

"Hi. It looks pretty dark over there, so I thought I'd check on you."

He sounded like the old Finn, which confused her. He'd been running hot and cold lately, to the point that she felt more comfortable not talking to him. "Thanks. I'm fine."

"Okay. Well, just so you know, when I moved back, I had a solar system installed."

"Which one? The Milky Way?"

Finn used his talking-to-a-two-year-old voice. "That's a galaxy, Annie."

"I know, I was just... never mind."

"Anyway, if that fails, I've still got the trusty, rusty old generator as a backup."

"Thanks, I'll manage."

"Do you have enough water?"

"Sure." She went to the sink, and nothing came out.

Finn said, "'Cause you know the well water can't pump without power, which means you won't be able to flush your toilet either—unless you've got a bucket of water."

"Oh." Not only was she going to freeze, but her whole house would smell like toilet while she dehydrated her way into hypothermia. *Lovely.* "Maybe it'll come back on soon."

Finn actually chuckled. He didn't even try to

hide it. "Look, Oakley, you can go full-on pioneer over there if you want, but just be aware I've got heat, water, more junk food than you could possibly dream of—and movies. The cable's out, too, by the way. But you won't miss it, because you don't have power."

"I'm low-tech. I read books."

"Okay. But if that Abe-Lincoln-reading-by-the-fire bit gets old, come on over."

"Thanks, Finn. I'll keep that in mind."

Two hours later, Annie was at Finn's door with a blanket, a pillow, Mr. Willoughby peeking over the top of an overnight bag, and a plate full of freshly made Christmas cookies. She knocked at the door.

He answered the door with a broad smile on his face. "What took you so long? Come on in."

If she had known cheerful Finn would answer the door, she would've come an hour sooner. She still didn't understand these moods of his lately, but she was happy to be in a warm cabin, so she set thoughts of Finn's moods aside.

The place was so toasty that she stood and soaked in the warmth for a moment.

"Are you okay?" He seemed genuinely concerned.

"I'm just so happy to be warm!"

The warmth in his cabin was nothing compared to the warmth in his eyes. Why did it always come back to this? It didn't matter how much time passed; he could still affect her. At the moment, he was doing it by putting his arms around her shoulders as he led her to the fire.

"We need to get you warmed up." He proceeded to rub her shoulders and arms and then moved to her hands. She wanted to offer her feet for a massage, but she exercised self-control and didn't ask. If she were forced to choose between giving up the wood stove or his arm about her, it would come down to survival or Finn. Why did she always choose Finn?

Countless times over the years, she had wondered how long it took to fall out of love. But as she sat in his cabin, feeling all safe and warm, she realized it was never going to happen. She would always love Finn. She'd begun to realize that in the bakery with Alex. He was exactly the sort of man she could fall in love with, but her heart was already taken. She'd convinced herself all these years she'd stayed single that it was for Ella. But if she had remarried, Ella would have been fine. But Annie would never be whole without Finn.

Annie lived in the real world, so she had to make do. But for now, it was snowing outside, and the real world looked like a winter wonderland. So she would enjoy being safe inside with the man she secretly loved. People say age gives you wisdom, but for Annie, it gave her the ability to live in the moment and appreciate it for what it was. So for now, she was having her perfect Christmas with Finn, and that was enough.

They spent the next hour toasting hot dogs over the fire with Finn's outdoor barbecue fork. Why had she never thought of that? They were delicious. Then Finn made popcorn over the fire in an antique fireplace popcorn popper that had belonged to his grandparents.

"You know you can do that in a microwave."

He stared at her as though she'd lost her mind. He made no attempt to hide his disdain. "Yeah, I guess you could if you didn't care what it tasted like. It's not the same without the little charred bits from the fireplace flames. Besides, Oakley, you don't get the same warm, cozy feel sitting and staring at the dots on your microwave door."

Annie kept her mouth closed and suppressed the laughter that was bubbling up. She didn't even say a word when he microwaved the butter to pour over the top.

With a mouthful of popcorn, she said, "Oh my gosh. This is really good."

He gave her an *I told you so* look, then they chose up sides of the sofa for the next event of the evening, the great movie battle. They went through a long list. *Little Women*—any version—was a hard no for Finn.

"In fact, nothing with Victorian costumes—or costumes in general."

"But—"

"Sorry, no."

They wound up agreeing on *Die Hard* with one stipulation. Annie said, "Do not think that we're going from that to *Lethal Weapon*, 'cause that's not gonna happen."

Finn protested. "Why not?"

"Well, for one thing, you can't start a Christmas movie with a guy trying to commit suicide."

Finn raised an eyebrow. "Four words: *It's a Wonderful Life.*"

Any wrinkled her nose. "Technically, that's five words, but point taken. Still..." She took the *Lethal Weapon* disc from him. "The answer is no."

He rolled his eyes. "Fine. We'll start with *Die Hard* and take it from there."

They shook on it and started the movie.

By the time the movie was finished, it was too early to call it a night but too late to start another movie, so Finn put on some soft Christmas music, poured them each an Irish cream liqueur, and plopped down on the sofa. "It's weird, isn't it? Being back here together?"

"I don't know if 'weird' is the right word, but we do seem to have come full circle."

Finn smiled to himself. "You know, sometimes I look over at your place and miss the way things used to be."

Nostalgia overwhelmed her. Finn had caught her off guard. "We grew up. We had lives of our own. To be honest, I never got the impression Georgina thought too much of me."

"She was jealous."

"What?" That was absurd.

"It was our friendship. We had something she and I never had."

Annie wasn't sure what to say. There were things she could say, but they would make matters worse. The last thing she wanted was to dredge up feelings she'd worked so hard to bury. Why was he doing this now?

"Georgina didn't understand that our friendship couldn't make the marriage any worse than it already was. I don't know why I'm telling you this." He smiled. "It's the liqueur talking. I guess I'm still getting over the divorce. Although it's not like it was a surprise. We both knew early on it wasn't working, but we were like the musicians on the *Titanic*. We just kept going as if nothing were wrong. Then she got pregnant, and I refused to be an absentee father. So here I am."

Why was he telling her this?

As if reading her mind, he explained. "We've never talked about certain parts of our lives. So I thought this was as good a time as any."

Since they were digging into the past, Annie went with it. She had questions of her own. Maybe she'd get some answers. "How did you know it was a mistake?"

A troubled look filled his eyes as he stared at the fire. "When I came here in the summers after I got married, seeing you was like looking through a window at a life that was gone. All that was left was crushing disappointment."

Annie's heart ached for him and for what he'd been through. "You always seemed happy." Not always, but she couldn't tell him about the times she'd watched him walk down to the creek as though something weighed heavily on him.

He smiled bitterly. "I was happiest here. It was all about Connor. I wanted my son to have the sort of memories I have of this place. He's why my marriage lasted as long as it did. All children deserve a happy childhood, no matter how unhappy their parents might be."

Annie knew she was in danger of saying too much, but she couldn't help herself. "I wish we could have talked then."

Finn's eyes bored through her. "That would not have been a good idea."

She almost asked him why not, but she knew. "I just mean that I could have used someone to talk to. You and I had grown distant. I couldn't talk to my parents—before or after Matt died. They wanted so much to believe I was fine that I couldn't disappoint them. When did the roles reverse so we don't want to tell our parents the truth any more than they wanted to tell us the truth about Santa Claus? So we all just pretend to be okay for each other's sake."

Finn stared at the fire. "I got so tired of trying to seem happy."

"Me too."

He turned and gazed into her eyes, and the pain she saw there was so deep, she thought she might drown. She averted her eyes.

Finn said, "Can I ask you a question?"

The fact that he'd asked permission made her

sure that she didn't want to answer, and yet she said, "Okay."

"Why didn't you ever remarry?"

She smiled through her sorrow. "I'd already made one mistake. I was better off alone than in a bad marriage, so I decided to focus on Ella."

She saw his questioning look and answered before he could ask. "I got lonely sometimes. I even got to a point where I hoped I'd meet someone, but I never did."

"You know, Annie, if you'd ever needed anything, I would have been there for you."

"I know."

"And that offer will stand until... I can't." He grinned.

"Same here."

"Annie, come here." She joined Finn at the window, where over a foot of snow had coated the lawn leading down to the creek. Snow-laden branches bowed down to the glowing moonlight. The night was so still, only the large flakes of snow dared to stir. It was as if life had paused to give Annie a sense of her bearings. It worked. In this moment, she felt completely at peace.

Finn broke the silence—and the peace. "What are you doing with Alex?"

The question came out of nowhere. "Alex?"

"I saw you together."

"At the bakery?" She narrowed her eyes.

"Have you been anywhere else together?"

She didn't like his tone, so she smirked. "Is this Finn the cop asking? Am I under arrest?"

"I was in town picking up supplies for the storm, and I walked past the bakery," he said. "There you were."

She knew that look. He was clearly upset, but she wasn't sure why. "We had coffee. No big deal."

"Big deals start with coffee."

Annie narrowed her eyes and smiled. "You should write ad slogans. Let's get Folgers on the line."

He snapped at her. "I'm not joking!"

"I thought you must be because otherwise, you're making no sense."

"What do you even know about him?"

"Well, for starters, he likes coffee." She couldn't help herself. She didn't understand why Finn was acting this way. Her knee-jerk response was to lighten the mood, but it seemed to be having the opposite effect.

"You just met him."

"Yes, because he's new in town. No one knows him—except Regi. And she introduced us. But you know that already because you were there."

"Regi! Now there's a great judge of character!"

"Well, she's got me as a friend, so yes, I'd say she is."

For someone so quick to criticize, he was suddenly quiet.

Annie said, "I like Alex. He's smart, kind, and..."

She almost said handsome, but she didn't think that would go over too well. "And he must be successful. He bought that stunning Victorian house I've always loved."

He turned in stunned disbelief. "So this is about a house?"

Annie was stupefied. "No, this is about coffee!" Was he really suggesting that she would strike up a relationship with a guy to get to his house?

Finn was relentless. "If he works in Albany, what's he doing up here?"

"The same thing any of us are doing. It's beautiful. Most of his work is remote, so he moved here because he can. What's wrong with that?" Annie had never seen Finn like this.

He seemed to calm down somewhat. "I just don't think... I didn't think you were looking to date anyone."

"I wasn't, but I could. But just to be clear, this wasn't a date. We ran into each other outside the bakery, and we sat down and had coffee. But I wouldn't mind going out with him—and I might. What's wrong with that?"

Jaw clenched, Finn stared straight ahead.

His annoyance was so bizarre that it amused her. She playfully nudged her shoulder against his.

Completely unaware of her attempts to make eye

contact, he fixed his gaze through the window, where the wind picked up and sent snow flying about. "Do you know how many times I've wished I had the chance to talk you out of marrying Matt? I refuse to make that mistake again."

Annie's jaw dropped. "You think I'm about to marry Alex?"

"Not this minute, no. But I can't stand by and watch another train wreck."

That hurt. He was probably right. Her marriage to Matt had been a train wreck, but it still hurt to hear it.

Finn shook his head. "Never mind. It's none of my business."

"Good point."

"Go ahead and repeat your mistakes."

If this had been anyone else, Annie would have just walked away. But this was Finn. There had to be a logical reason he was badgering her, but she sure couldn't see it from where she was. "First of all, if I haven't been clear, this was coffee. But, yes, I think he's interested in me. Go figure! There's no accounting for taste. But for you to compare Alex to Matt—"

"I love you."

That knocked the wind out of her.

Annie couldn't believe this was happening. If she

could, she would be happy. Finn had just said he loved her. But instead of filling her heart with love, it felt like he'd ripped open a wound—one that had never quite healed.

He turned to her. "I've loved you since right after college."

"Well, that makes sense. I should've known that when you went off to Europe with that girl."

"Why do you think I came back early from Europe? I know I told you I came back because I missed you. The whole truth is that I realized I loved you."

"I don't believe you, because I loved you. And if you loved me back, I would've known."

"Not if I was a jerk."

She stared at the swirling snow and muttered, "I can't argue with that." She couldn't bring herself to look at him. This was all too much. She didn't know what to think, let alone what to do.

Finn shook his head slowly. "I came back, and you'd already run off with Matt. You were married. I've spent my life wishing I could have stopped you."

Now she was scared—scared to hear one more word. Scared to have hope. Scared most of all to give in to what her heart wanted.

"Annie, look at me."

She felt as though she were moving in slow

motion. She struggled to turn and look into his eyes. *Please don't hurt me.*

"Annie. I love you. I don't want to lose you again."

She said, "I loved you. But when you left for Europe, I knew you didn't love me. And then I met Matt. He swept me off my feet. He was the antidote to you. I thought I'd be cured. I'd be happy. Obviously, that didn't work out according to plan."

Finn sighed. "I'm not thrilling like Matt or charming like Alex. I'm just the guy next door who's always loved you but didn't get it at first. But I do love you, Annie."

He brushed a loose strand of hair from her forehead. He barely touched her, but it made her pulse race. He leaned closer until she thought he would hear her heart pound. His gaze softened, and she felt herself lean toward him. He took her face in his hands.

"Oakley."

His lips touched hers, gently at first, then his lips parted and his kiss grew more urgent. Annie slipped her arms about his neck while he wrapped his arms around her waist. His palm pressed the small of her back, and she gave in completely to that kiss. She didn't want it to end. But it did, and he kissed her again. For most of her life, she had dreamed of his kiss, but she never imagined how the mere touch of his lips could make her head spin and her body feel like a fireworks display. He pulled away just enough to gaze into her eyes with a warmth that spread through her.

"Finn Burton." She felt as though she had to say it to confirm it was happening, then she kissed him again.

Outside, the large flakes of snow floated down like they had been all day. Inside, the fire in the wood stove crackled and filled the cabin with its usual warmth. But Annie and Finn's world had changed.

Finn and Annie stayed up talking most of the night. When the power came on in the morning, Annie went home to get some sleep. That wasn't easy. She had so much to think of, and her heart was so full. But she managed a few hours before she got up and started cooking. She still couldn't quite believe her perfect Christmas had turned into something she'd never dared dream of.

Finn came over in the late afternoon for a Christmas Eve dinner. She'd always known life could be this happy for others. She just never believed it would be for her. After dinner, Annie started to clear the table, but before she could stand, Finn touched her hand to stop her. "This is so new. It still feels so fragile. I want to give you all the time that you need, but—brace yourself, Oakley. I know it sounds kind of sudden after more than two decades—but I'll probably love you forever." He was quietly certain.

Peace settled as gently as new falling snow. She and Finn were in love. It was simple and true.

Annie pressed her lips to his. This was the man she had loved all her life. By the time the kiss ended, they were wrapped in each other's arms in the midst of a world full of promise. Christmas Eve was a time of new beginnings, and this Christmas was theirs.

At last, now she knew. This would be the year Finn loved her back.

EPILOGUE

Christmas Eve, five years later

Finn opened the door for Regi and Alex. Annie rushed to join them. "Merry Christmas!"

When the greetings and hugs were all finished, they'd barely made it the few steps to the great room when Regi said, "I can't wait any longer. Look at this!"

She held out her left hand, which boasted a new brilliant blue tanzanite ring. "We're engaged!"

Annie hugged Regi. "I'm so happy for you!" And she was. Years before, Regi's boyfriend had dumped her in miserable fashion on New Year's Eve. Alex saw her through the breakup, first as friends then eventually more. By then, Finn had come around to appreciate Alex for the upstanding guy that he was—

especially when he wasn't a rival for Annie's
affections.

Finn opened a bottle of champagne to celebrate
the engagement and was just handing Regi her glass
when they heard a car pull up and park in the
driveway.

Annie pulled on her coat and went out to greet
their new guests. Connor and Ella were just barely
out of the car when a four-year-old brunette hopped
out and ran down the walkway to Annie and Finn.

"Charlotte! Slow down." Ella shrugged helplessly. Her daughter was already in her grandmother's arms. When Charlotte was done hugging Annie,
Finn picked up his granddaughter and carried her
into the cottage.

Charlotte said, "Wait!" Finn stopped in the
doorway so Charlotte could reach up and touch the
horseshoe.

Annie said, "You know, my grandmother—your
great-great-grandmother—once told me that the first
one to pass under this horseshoe gets to make a wish."

"Put me down, Grandpa." Charlotte ran halfway
up the walkway and then ran back under the horseshoe and into the cottage. "I made a wish. When will
it come true?"

Annie and Finn exchanged glances. She said, "It
might take a long time."

Charlotte's eyebrows furrowed, but Annie continued, "But this one's a Christmas wish, and I believe Christmas wishes are worth waiting for."

BOOK NEWS

Would you like to know when the next book comes out? Click below to sign up for the J.L. Jarvis Journal and get book news, free books, and exclusive content delivered monthly.

news.jljarvis.com

ACKNOWLEDGMENTS

Thanks to Bridget B. Walker, MD for sharing her
medical expertise.

Editing by Red Adept Editing
redadeptediting.com

ABOUT THE AUTHOR

J.L. Jarvis is a left-handed opera singer/teacher/lawyer who writes books. She now lives and writes in upstate New York.

Sign up to be notified of book releases and related news:
news.jljarvis.com

Email JL at:
writer@jljarvis.com

Follow JL online at:
jljarvis.com

facebook.com/jljarvis1writer

twitter.com/JLJarvis_writer

instagram.com/jljarvis.writer

bookbub.com/authors/j-l-jarvis

pinterest.com/jljarviswriter

goodreads.com/5106618.J_L_Jarvis

amazon.com/author/B005G0M2Z0

youtube.com/UC7kodjlaG-VcSZWhuYUUl_Q

Made in the USA
Las Vegas, NV
18 February 2022

44198961R00132